THE DAY WE MET

The very first day
of long-term relationships

Edited by Jack Hart

ALYSON PUBLICATIONS
LOS ANGELES

Manufactured in the United States of America.
Printed on acid-free paper.

This trade paperback original is published by Alyson Publications Inc.,
P.O. Box 4371, Los Angeles, California 90078-4371.
Distribution in the United Kingdom by Turnaround Publisher Services Ltd.,
Unit 3 Olympia Trading Estate, Coburg Road, Wood Green,
London N22 6TZ, England.

First edition: October 1996

10 9 8 7 6 5 4 3 2 1

ISBN 1-55583-352-7

Credits
    A version of "Potluck Surprise" by Peter House appeared in the May 1992
issue of *The Empty Closet.*
    A version of "A Weekend That Lasted Forever" by Walter R. Ruzycki
appeared in the November/December 1994 issue of *Spectrum Senior News.*

CONTENTS

AFTER MIDNIGHT
by Kelvin Beliele

I first saw Dennis in the summer of 1969 — the country was still reeling from the deaths of Martin Luther King Jr. and Robert Kennedy, we'd been shocked by the Democratic National Convention in Chicago, and a leatherman had appeared on the cover of *Life* magazine.

Robert, a straight friend of mine from high school, and Dennis were college hippies in my small hometown. In that era it seemed that we all shared a certain sense of community, unspoken alliances that centered around the war in Vietnam, civil rights, and personal freedom.

Dennis and Mike, another of the roommates in their hippie house, were shopping in the clothing store I worked in. Dennis and I cruised each other, smiling, barely speaking. I studied Dennis as he waited outside the fitting room for Mike. I was shy, Mike was in a hurry, and I had other customers, but I liked Dennis's presence and the way we watched each other. His image stayed with me long after that day: his large, sad eyes; his kissable lips; his slender torso; and his tight jeans.

We weren't formally introduced until New Year's Eve, 1969 — well, actually, shortly after midnight, during the first hours of 1970. We were in Robert's house, and there among the black-light posters and the makeshift furnishings, Robert introduced me to Dennis. He was still beautiful and sensual, his bell-bottoms tight in the crotch, a strand of blue love beads around his neck. I was entranced by his full lips and his big basket. It was as if Dennis and I were alone in the room, in the world. He watched me, and I in turn was able only to gaze back, the desire and wonder filling me. I was floating away on romantic, poetic ideals of love and two men together.

Later, at the all-night truck stop, over burgers and Cokes, Robert told me, "Dennis is bisexual, you know." Even as naive and provincial as I was, I knew that *bisexual* easily translated to *gay*. I had a chance with Dennis! And the rest of that night, even after I was alone at my parents' house, I thought of him, of touching him, talking with him, living with him…

I returned to college after the winter break and didn't see him again for months. All that while, I thought of him and hoped that he was thinking of me. After all, he was the older man, wise and sophisticated. He was twenty-one, and I was eighteen.

In May 1970, during finals week, Robert and his friends visited — and Dennis too! He was still wearing tight hip-huggers, and his harness boots fairly shone. We talked for a long time, thriving on being together, touching, talking, laughing, being in love immediately. I knew why I was gay. I had waited all my life for him. We fell right into step with each other.

When we were finally alone in my room, we began undressing each other, and the wonder of being alone like that with a man I liked, maybe was in love with, overcame me. I ran my hands along his slender warm body, and I knew that he was just as thrilled, just as eager to please and to be pleased as I was. And when we toppled onto that lumpy mattress on that rickety bedstead, I knew that he was the man I wanted. I was at home with this gawky, intelligent, sensitive hippie boy. And I knew, deep in my heart, as we curled into each other, that he was at home with me. Now, more than twenty-five years later, we still are — still in love, still filled with wonder and desire, and still at home with each other.

LET'S DANCE
by Robert Cataldo

I met Roger one hot August night at the 1270, a gay bar in Boston. He was standing at the edge of the dance floor, and I, likewise, just across from him. He had dark curly hair — too much like my own, I remember thinking — and dark, deep-set eyes. He was thin, about my own height, and at least my own age.

As he had been standing there for quite some time, I figured he might want to dance. I walked over and gave him a sidelong glance. I don't think he even noticed me standing next to him. "Would you like to dance?" I asked. He nodded. I was relieved and happy, and we walked off. It was a fast disco song; the floor was crowded, and I remember repeatedly trying to catch his eye, but he had this annoying habit of looking just past me.

Unsure, disappointed, beaten, I thanked him for the dance and walked him back. He didn't say anything, and I went downstairs to have a beer. I was hurt and a little angry and tried to convince myself that it wouldn't matter if he weren't there when I got back. After a cigarette or two, I walked back to the dance floor. He was still standing there. I wasn't keen on being rejected, and he hadn't met anyone either, so, a little woozy from the beer, I asked, "Would you like to dance again?" He nodded.

With the tight crowd, it wasn't difficult to dance close. I put one arm around his shoulder, leaned close, and held him; all the while he was singing the lyrics to a song by the Emotions in my ear. I could feel his warm body through my shirt.

We wandered off the dance floor on the pitiful excuse that I had to pee. As I stepped out, however, Roger walked past me. "I'm going to the ice machine," he said, and I nodded. When he came back, he popped two fingers and an ice cube in my mouth. He smiled. It was the most encouraging thing that had happened to me all night.

It was late, and the crowd was as thick as ever. He mentioned that he still had his two drink tickets and offered to give me one. "Really?" I said. "Let's go downstairs." I thought the lesbian bar in the basement would be the least crowded.

We sat and talked, and he told me a little about himself. He was from Woonsocket, Rhode Island, an old mill town that was home to one of the oldest gay bars in the country. He was living, however, at the University of Rhode Island in Kingston, about an hour south of Providence, and when I asked where he was staying, he said, "Nowhere, really. The Y."

I wasn't sure if he wanted to come home with me. I wasn't sure if he wanted me to ask. I was a little drunk and and a little scared. He didn't say anything, but we touched fingers once or twice. I figured he wanted me to say something, and I did. "Would you like to come home with me?" I asked. "I don't live far."

He thought about it for a few seconds. "Where did you say you live?" he asked.

"On St. Botolph Street. We can walk from here."

"I guess it'd be all right."

I was still undecided, however. I had been in three major relationships and too many minor ones over the past few years. But it was an August night, hot and dry, the leaves rustling faintly in the breeze, my new friend walking cheerfully by my side. He made me feel older and wiser and made me recall all the innocence I had lost.

I was walking there by his side, lost in my own thoughts, when I heard him sing "Frank Mills," an old funny song from *Hair* that I thought I knew. "I met a boy called Frank Mills on September twelfth right here in front of the Waverly..." He knew all the lyrics. I joined in where I could: "I love him but it embarrasses me to walk down the street with him. He lives in Brooklyn somewhere and wears a white crash helmet..." It was funny and sweet and sad, and I knew he was singing it just for me.

My bedroom was long and narrow, with a small window behind the bed. Exhausted, I undressed and fell into bed. I avoided putting on the overhead blue light — I didn't want any reminders of past romances. There was city light coming in through the kitchen windows, so it wasn't entirely dark.

I remember feeling very happy and tired and a little drunk. I lay back and watched my little friend get undressed. He was modest and wore a pair of dark blue bikini briefs to come to bed. I didn't have a stitch on. As he pulled back the covers, however, I noticed that his sweet little tummy had no fat at all. With his dark curly hair, he looked like a sculpture of a Greek boy just come to life; he seemed pure and innocent. It was the second most delightful thing about him that night.

I'm sure I made the first move. He was all elbows and knees, and the blue bikini briefs were the first to go. He felt good and sweet, and when I wasn't punctured by an elbow or a knee, it seemed to me we were a good fit. He didn't fight me off; half asleep, we made love.

He came to stay with me for three weekends before I moved. I had been a cook at some good restaurants months before, so the first weekend I made chicken Cordon Bleu (and starved all week); the second, stuffed sole with crab. But by the third week, we were reduced to spaghetti sauce. Fortunately for me, he told me red sauce was his favorite. My mother always said, "Find a man who's easy to cook for," but I was the only one of my siblings, I guess, who listened.

After seventeen years Roger and I have had our ups and downs, but his sweetness and body temperature have remained the same. I have no idea what day in August 1977 it was when we first met. We celebrate our anniversary on August 15, the only holiday to fall in late summer, the Assumption of the Virgin Mary into heaven, when she was "assumed," body and soul. He calls it the Erection!

SWEET SONG
by Wayne Fritsche

I was a new member of the Boston Gay Men's Chorus, and Curt was a veteran of three years. At my first rehearsal I found a place in the baritone section to sit, and Curt leaned forward to ask whether I would like to borrow his sheet music. (New members hadn't yet received several of that season's pieces.) I thanked him and took note of his face — friendly and cute in a bookish sort of way.

Later that evening we began to practice one of the pieces Curt had lent me, "Sometimes When We Touch." (No, this has not become our song.) As we neared the end of the song, I noticed that the last page was missing, a problem for someone who'd never seen this music before in his life. I turned around and said to Curt, "I think you're missing something," and gestured toward the music. He leaned forward and, in what seemed like a complete non sequitur, began to explain how one section of the song called for the baritones to split and sing different lines of music. I had no idea what any of this had to do with the missing last page, but I pretended I understood and continued singing. We soon reached the missing page, and I finally said to Curt, "You're missing the last page of this song!"

A lightbulb went off for him, and he explained, "Oh! I thought you were telling me that I was singing the wrong notes!" I was mortified that this experienced singer thought a new member like me would dare to criticize him and said so with all the humility I could muster.

At the break I did my best to mingle, although I knew only a handful of the other members. I had heard that it was a chorus tradition to go out to a bar called Fritz after rehearsals, so my brilliant opening line of small talk with Curt was, "So, are you going to Fritz tonight?" One of my fellow chorus members, John, noticed Curt and I standing near each other and said, "Wayne, you and Curt should talk. He went to Dartmouth, and you went to Williams, and those are pretty close to each other." This would be true only if there were no state of Vermont, but it was a conversation starter. Curt now insists that I used my line about going to Fritz on him not once but twice. I deny it vehemently, of course, but Curt began to think I might be interested in him and resolved to go to Fritz even though he was exhausted and had planned to go home.

When the rehearsal ended I actually thought I would go straight home as well because I was an insecure 24-year-old who didn't much like large crowds of strangers or gay bars. Curt, however, thought I was just playing coy. He and John each grabbed an arm and forced me out the door, and off to Fritz we went.

At the bar Curt and I had the opportunity to chat at length. He bought me a drink, and we learned how much we had in common even though ten years separated us: degrees in English, lots of sisters (Curt four and me three), experience living in England, and massive crushes on Prince

Edward. At several points other members tried to get in on the conversation, but Curt and I were much more focused on getting to know each other than on mixing.

By the end of the evening, when we exchanged numbers and Curt gave me a ride home, Curt was hooked and I was intrigued. I am much more Curt's "type" than he is mine, but I was drawn in by the pleasure of his company, his open and engaging manner, his sense of humor, and his sweet disposition. I hoped the exchange of numbers meant we'd have the opportunity to meet outside of rehearsal.

The next day, my phone rang, and some intuition led me to allow the answering machine to get the call. Sure enough, it was Curt asking me to dinner before the next rehearsal. I did a little pirouette, waited twenty minutes, and called him back as though I'd just gotten home. We began a courtship that lasted a full month before we actually slept together. With many more years of experience than I had, Curt was much more ready to embark on a sexual and emotional relationship than I was; nevertheless, he treated me with absolute respect and godlike patience and gradually won my heart, my body, and my soul.

This was three and a half years ago, and with each passing day we grow closer and more deeply in love. Of course, this was the first long-term commitment for both of us, so I do sometimes wonder what it would be like to be involved with someone else. But while I may occasionally fantasize about spending my life with other men — usually rich, beautiful, and unavailable men — I can't imagine not spending it with Curt. He remains the most important person in the world to me and the most beautiful man I've ever known.

GREAT SCOT

by Hyde

I flew to Scotland at the request of an old friend of mine. Denny had gone home to Paisley to be near his mother after he'd become ill. Unexpectedly, she died before him, and he was left alone. He wasn't so sick that he needed nursing care, but he had reached a stage where living alone wasn't the best idea. Knowing my "why not?" attitude toward life, he asked me to stay with him.

I had a job at a Connecticut rare book library at the time, handling precious volumes all day. It was the best position I'd ever held and for once I got cold feet about resigning. On second thoughts, though, my job simply entailed shelving those books and monitoring the reading room. It was all perfectly pleasant, even wonderful at times, yet there was hardly a career in it for me. Whereas with Denny's proposition, real-life experiences were beckoning. Predictably, I called Denny back and said yes – or rather, "Why not?"

Denny met me at Prestwick Airport, taking full advantage of his handicap sticker by parking nearly at the arrival gate.

We took a drive through the Ayr countryside and a leisurely tour of Glasgow before heading home to Paisley.

The morning after arriving, while still getting settled into my rooms (with typical Scots generosity Denny had fixed up a bedroom and a small studio in his not overly large highrise flat), I met Denny's odd-job man, Peter.

Peter at the time was a resourceful, industrious, and impish fourteen-year-old who lived in the flat immediately above ours with his parents and two brothers. Always willing to vacuum the carpets, wash windows, make a trip down to the shops ("doing the messages," in the local dialect), or otherwise make himself useful for the odd pound or two, Peter was an indispensable help to Denny. He was the kind of energetic and sociable boy who you knew would gladly have gone on helping had Denny run low on pocket money.

Peter was a good kid, and a cute kid, but a kid nonetheless, and I treated him accordingly, with a friendly reserve appropriate for someone of my relatively adult stature. (I was all of twenty-two myself).

When I learned he had an elder brother of eighteen, I pictured a slightly older and perhaps spottier version of Peter himself and thought no more about it.

During the second weekend of my stay, young Peter phoned from a little town on the Ayrshire coast explaining that he and his friend Alex missed their ride home after some event and hadn't the money for a bus. He asked if Denny would be willing to drive down and collect them. Denny was always game for a drive, so after the requisite grousing (for he was trying, though nobody would take him seriously, to cultivate at age thirty-two a reputation as a crabby old man), he said to Peter, "Aye, I'll come, but you'll work for free tomorrow."

As we drove back through town after picking up the boys,

Peter reached over from the backseat and began madly tooting the horn.

"What in—?" Denny demanded in hardly feigned outrage.

"There's James! There's James!" Peter crowed, waving to a gaggle of pedestrian youths with lordly disdain.

As we were momentarily held up behind a driver making an inept U-turn, I had time to ask Peter which one was his brother.

"He's the prat with the stickey."

"The stickey?" I repeated as we pulled away again.

"He's the young man with the cast on his arm," Denny translated.

I looked back. "Oh," I said, "the blond one with the deep-set eyes."

Curiosity about the eccentric Yank downstairs (somehow I got this reputation) brought James calling soon after, ostensibly to help his brother move Denny's aquarium.

James and I ended up doing the lifting – under Peter's loud and manic supervision – and Denny poured a cold drink for everyone afterward. In the half hour I spent in his company on that first visit, James and I barely said ten words to each other.

Slim and pretty short with an elegant, athletic build; soft green eyes of remarkable penetration; a smattering of light freckles; well-defined but not too sharp features, James was my ideal, the more so as I got to know him. Peter was still in school, of course, but James had dropped out during his final year. He didn't have a full-time job, but he wasn't a layabout. Nor was he by any means ignorant. It was simply the custom in their blue-collar neighborhood to leave school and commence adult life at that age.

Though James signed on to collect unemployment every other week, he'd give this money (no more than a pittance) to his mother to cover the cost of his board. For pocket money he worked on Fridays at a warehouse expediting the deliveries that had to go out before the weekend, which is how he'd broken an arm. He was hoping to be taken on full-time at the warehouse before long, but he held on to the notion that perhaps life might have more to offer him than had been available to his basically happy but decidedly thwarted parents, uncles, and aunts.

As he needed just enough money to knock around on the weekend a bit, he seemed to require a minimum quota of responsibility in his life. Thus, he'd assumed charge of the housekeeping for his parents, both of whom worked, and afternoons he kept an eye on Malachy, his youngest brother, after school let out. Yet his various jobs and concerns didn't begin to fully occupy him, and James had a lot of time on his hands. Intrigued by me, he started coming down to visit us every day once the chores upstairs in his parents' flat had been completed.

Initially, I felt it was something of a bother, an intrusion almost, having James hanging around so much. Denny took up a considerable chunk of my time, so between the two of them, I was kept so distracted that I wasn't doing justice to my own pursuits – my painting and my studies.

James tied flies as a hobby and as a little business catering to local fly-fisherman. I made the seemingly altruistic suggestion that he bring down all his equipment, and Denny cleared table space for him to set up. This kept him from being underfoot to some extent but, even so, he could sell only so many flies, and before long he'd built up a considerable backlog.

I couldn't rely on Denny to entertain our visitor either. He was a nocturnal insomniac – at night he'd prowl, unable to get a wink, and then to compensate he'd spend most of the day in bed. I might have had a word with James, ask that he only come down maybe three days a week for, say, an hour or two at a time. However, I was incapable of that kind of social confrontation. Besides, James was an undemanding, self-sufficient, quiet, and amusing guest. If I'd had all the time in the world, I would never have bridled at spending most every afternoon in his company.

When matters changed I can't pinpoint, but gradually I began to anticipate James's arrival as I drank my mid-morning coffee. Days when he hadn't knocked at our door by eleven o'clock, I found myself preoccupied with wondering what could be keeping him. If he hadn't come down or phoned before the delivery of Denny's meals-on-wheels at noon, I'd go upstairs to investigate.

He'd spend three or four evenings a week with us as well. I found, as the weeks went by, that I was progressively disappointed when the hour rolled around for him to go upstairs. Often we'd play cards or board games with Denny and a few of James's pals. Taking hikes was another great pastime, and a few times a week we'd go to the public swimming pool. But we were also content to quietly read or play backgammon, complete in each other's company. Eventually I found that rather than hindering my painting and my studies, having James around enlivened and renewed the significance of everything.

I understood just how attached I'd become to him when he and his family took a trip to Corfu. To fill the void one night, I drank most of the half-barrel of lager we'd been brewing together in Denny's kitchen, though I knew perfectly well the stuff was far from ready. Coming down from that drunk, I realized for the first time the extent of my...well, my love for James.

Denny, no longer himself in those last days, rather helped matters to progress when he noticed and began indulging in jealous, passive-aggressive sideswipes at the fledgling relationship. The tension eventually got James and I talking. I explained that Denny and I weren't lovers but that, yes, I am gay. Wonder of wonders, James proceeded to come out to me too.

Denny died early that winter. I'd long overstayed my visa by that time and hadn't the resources to set up a home away from home when the local council commenced to requisitioning the flat. I had to return to the States not long after Denny's funeral. Flying under the auspices of a church-organized package tour, James followed me three months later.

We have it stashed in the file cabinet somewhere, but most likely his return ticket has expired by now. He's been living here for eight years.

These days James is pushing for us to move to New York, while I'd like to return to Scotland. For the time being, though, we make our home in Philadelphia, the two of us and our beagle, Denny.

BUDDY
by K.R.B.

North Carolina is my home, but my mother comes from Kentucky. While I was growing up, my folks had frequent occasion to run back and forth across the Southern highlands visiting kith and kin. I graduated from high school in the spring of 1937, in the middle of the depression and under the ominous thunder of approaching war. However, atypical though it was for farm families, my parents never wavered from the expectation that I would go to college. They devoutly believed that, somehow, "God will provide for him who works to help himself." In that vein Mother insisted I take typing and shorthand. "It'll come in handy in college and might even help to earn your living," she had said.

My major high school activity was writing for the school newspaper and theater group. My mother saw a notice in our church paper of an essay contest and suggested I submit a piece. I did so and won an honorable mention. More important for me, the award came to the attention of a relative in the admissions office at a small church college in London, Kentucky. I was sent an application form to fill out and return, which I did. In due course I was admitted and offered a work-study scholarship. That meant I was guaranteed a student job for which I'd get no money, but my tuition would be waived — not a small thing back then. With no reluctance I went to Kentucky, secretly glad to be out of the nest and on my own. Relatives were instructed to check on me and admonish any wandering from the straight and narrow path. Fortunately, there was mutual aversion to supervision, and nothing came of that.

Going to a distant school where everyone and everything is strange was disquieting for a country boy who had grown up with and known all his classmates since kindergarten. A childhood illness left me with a slight disability — not one to prevent ordinary physical activity but enough to rule out participation in competitive sports. My desire for some kind of student recognition pushed me into academics. During my entire freshman year, I was the classic grind — no social life, no extracurricular activities, no friends, but near the top in every course I took and on the dean's list all three quarters. I was the complete introvert.

In diametric contrast to me was Perry Lawrence. He was from an old, politically connected, horsey family from Lexington-Bardstown bluegrass country. In the meeting of the incoming class of '41, he was elected president of the freshman class. His guileless interest in people, social grace, irrepressible sense of humor, creative ingenuity, physical energy, and basic good looks made him totally irresistible to men and women alike. He had every right to be conceited. Whenever a leader was needed, everyone thought of Perry, and he was incapable of saying no to anyone. Consequently he was involved in dozens of activities: student government, drama club, cheerleading, tennis, swimming, and track, to name only a few. He had many irons in the fire, but grades weren't his big thing. I knew who Perry was from my first day on campus but had no personal contact with him during my entire first year.

My work-study assignment was at the college library. The portable Royal typewriter my parents had given me as a high school graduation present, along with my newly acquired secretarial skills, qualified me for a job cataloging new books and magazines for fifteen hours a week. I was given a small alcove deep in the library basement close to the rear delivery entrance, where books were deposited for accession. I was able to use the space as a personal study carrel, the perfect nest for a dedicated scholar.

It was hard times for Southern farmers in the late '30s, so I looked around for a way to take some of the burden of my education off my folks. The Presbyterian church across the street from campus had a position open for a live-in custodian. Usually it was given to a religion and philosophy major, but none had applied. I jumped at the chance and was given the job. It consisted of opening and locking up the facility for midweek meetings, setting up chairs in conference rooms, things like that, but no regular janitorial work. As custodian, I was given a bedroom with a double bed, desk, and easy chair and an adjoining bath. The room originally had been designed to accommodate visiting clergy but proved to be inadequate for that purpose.

With my tuition and room free, I still needed a cash job to give me pocket money. My cash-flow problem was solved a few weeks into the first term when I heard of, applied for, and got a job in the pathology lab at the municipal hospital. It involved the daily cleaning and sterilization of test tubes, culture dishes, specimen bottles, and the like. I was paid five dollars a week. The lab director, a WAC-type senior technician and nurse, said they wanted the work done right and that I should expect to spend about three hours a day at the job. She didn't care when I worked — morning, afternoon, or night was OK — just so it was done right. The job was a piece of cake. It took less than a week to learn all the ropes, including running the autoclave. It only took a little over an hour each day after I worked out my system and made sure to come after closing time so as to avoid interruptions and the yak-yak-yak of technicians. Every minute of my day had a name on it. There was little time for goofing off.

In the fall of 1938, I came back to college with essentially the same job and room setup as before. As a typical sophomore, I was far more self-confident and sure of myself than when I arrived as a freshman. It was flattering to be recognized by many more classmates than I expected would remember me. One of them was Perry. He greeted me with a radiant smile and said, "Hi, Ken. How was your summer in Granite Springs? I see on the class lists we're taking two courses together, Western Civilization and Art History. Maybe we can get together and study sometime."

Awed by his presence, I was too tongue-tied to mumble a reply. Then, like a butterfly, he was off hailing someone else, swept away by the crowd.

Although filled with a warm glow by his recognition, I realistically knew it was only momentary cordiality possibly triggered by the need for a cram-session partner at test time. Whatever the motive, his condescension made my day. The warmth of his grin and personal reference to my hometown in North Carolina showed he really did know who I was. I was won over instantly. How handsome he was, how well his thin freckled nose set off his curly auburn hair and flashing brown eyes.

Two days later, on the first day of classes, Perry was waiting outside the Western Civ. auditorium. He motioned me aside and said, "It's open seating, but we must continue to use the seats we choose. It's a large class, so let's try for places on the central aisle about halfway down."

I nodded my head and said, "I'd like that." In Art History we were assigned seats alphabetically so, although we saw each other in class, we didn't sit together. After class we often went to the student union to talk. When we were better acquainted, Perry said a lot of guys thought I was a snobbish, curve-breaking grade snatcher, but he knew that, although I was a brain, I was just shy. He figured I'd never try to make his acquaintance, and that was why he took the initiative to get to know me. I explained about my jobs, how I didn't think anybody noticed me, and how there was no occasion for me to be snobbish to anyone, much less him. Perry said he had his eye on me all last year and wanted to be friends. I'd no idea why, since he already had more friends than God.

Perry introduced me into his circle of associates, and slowly I was accepted and absorbed into many campus activities that otherwise would have been closed to me. We often studied together, and not only for exams. he was involved in so many activities, his room was like Grand Central Station and only rarely suitable for study. Guys were always coming and going, and bull sessions often lasted far into the night. His roommate was a senior prelaw major who could talk the proverbial balls off real brass monkeys even when no one was around to listen. When Perry wanted to get away from all that ruckus, he'd come to my carrel in the library or to my room in the church. At first it wasn't a regular thing, but he knew he had a monastic refuge whenever he needed one. Gradually his visits became more frequent. We became close friends. Even though I was aware of the growing physical attraction I had for him, our relationship remained only intellectual and social. At study breaks we'd make coffee and shoot the breeze, mostly about movies, student activities, theater, arts, coursework, ambitions, goals — different things young men dream about to change the world. Perry was far more concerned with human rights causes than I. To him, creativity, freedom, ethics, truth, and justice were issues to live by and die for. He'd rail at me until I either told him to hush so I could study or left for one of my jobs. His parting shot usually was, "Kenny, you know I'm right!"

I knew I was falling ever more deeply in love with Perry. I tried to submerge my feelings but had little success in quenching my desire to touch and hold him in altogether unpermitted ways. For him to be so near and yet unobtainable in any meaningful way was becoming unbearable. I knew Perry liked me as a friend. He was far more perceptive than I about other people's feelings, and he may have guessed my thoughts about him. But I had no inkling of how he might react if I revealed my deep emotional attachment and sexual desire for him.

The first time anything physical happened between us came during exam week just before Christmas break in our sophomore year, 1938. Perry's roommate finished at midyear, and his close friends, including Perry but not me, took him to dinner at an "off limits" roadhouse on the Manchester Pike. When I got back to my room after the library closed, I found someone sleeping in my bed. It was Perry, of course, absolutely smashed. He'd come to study for tomorrow afternoon's exam but now was sound asleep and far removed from the possibility of any intellectual improvement. His clothes were strewn about, and he was buried under the covers. I considered my choices: Wake him? For what purpose? Get him back to his room? Out of the question. Let him stay? Good thinking! Sleep together in my bed? No other option open. That decided, I undressed, put on pajamas, and doused the lights.

He was sprawled out on his stomach, so I had to move him to make room for myself. I tentatively reached out to caress his naked shoulders and back. My body trembled with excitement, and I sprung a rod. I didn't know what to do next. He moaned, turned on his side, and with a melting smile repeated the old Vaudeville gag, "I'm not so think as you drunk I am." He put a hand on my chest and moved it up to pat my cheek gently. "I'm so glad we're here doing this. I've wanted to and waited so long. I was afraid you might reject and hate me." He unbuttoned my pajama shirt, pulled the pants string, and said, "We won't need these." I removed my night clothes. He put a leg between mine as I drew him into the circle of my arms. Our dicks throbbed together. We experimented with kisses and caresses. Our bodies strained together, and both of us came. After cleaning up, we held each other through the night. It was heaven.

For the remainder of that school year, although we spent much of our free time together, we weren't actually roommates. Perry kept his dormitory room and shared it with an incoming transfer student, a jock. The jock was OK but nothing special in the way of looks or brains and totally straight as far as I could tell. Perry and I were discreet. Externally there was no evidence of any change in our relationship. Everyone already knew that we were best friends, but only we know how truly great our friendship had become.

On several weekends that spring Perry took me to visit his folks in Bloomfield, near Bardstown. His granddaddy said I was a good influence on Buddy (the family pet name for Perry) for helping him study. He said, "Buddy is a flibbertigibbet. He's interested in too many things. He has a good mind but needs to settle on something and master it." He approved of me even more when I said I'd often suggested to Perry that he include prelaw prerequisites in his electives so he'd be ready to move in that direction if, eventually, he decided to go into politics. Before year's end Perry convinced his folks that he needed an off-campus apartment for his junior and senior years so he could do more studying. Granddaddy said, "I'll pay for it if Buddy has the good judgment to ask that nice young man with his head screwed on straight (meaning me) to share the place and ride herd on him."

Our last two years, sharing an off-campus apartment, were about as idyllic as college can be. We lived together in harmony unfettered in opportunities to enjoy our youthful powers for sexual expression without in the least detracting from our other activities. I continued to work toward my collegiate goals. Perry was volatile and swung from transient summits of creative euphoria to chasms of self-doubt. I believe I was good for him as a buffer against both emotional extremes. My love and admiration for him grew with my understanding of his moods, of the scope of his creativity, of his sincere concern for human liberties, of his zest for life.

Perry finally put his act together. He was voted Big Man on Campus for our school and is listed in the National Collegiate Record of 1941 as one of the nation's best. He was admitted to the University of Virginia law school. His launching pad was cocked and ready to fire. But the war put an end to all that.

Both of us were drafted, I for limited service owing to my physical disability. I played a pedestrian role in "saving the world for democracy" by being assigned to Ordinance, where I pushed papers designed to ensure that wooden ammunition crates would be sufficiently buoyant to float ashore in the event they were cast overboard at sea.

Perry had to be in the thick of things, and nothing but the

Navy would do. The following March I received a card saying he'd finished officer training and would be assigned to the carrier Yorktown. On May 6, 1942, the Yorktown was repeatedly hit by Japanese aerial bombs in the Battle of the Coral Seas. Perry now sleeps with thirty thousand comrades in Honolulu's Punch Bowl Crater, the National Military Cemetery of the Pacific. His grave is shaded by a great flamboyant flame tree that blooms each summer in remembrance of a rocket's red glare.

TASTY DESSERT
Anonymous

I was once more on summer vacation from my job as a high school English teacher in the Southwest and I had, as so often before, rented a cabin in the same isolated and inexpensive rural subdivision of the Big Island, the Orchid Isle. My brother visited here once — my brother the bigot, sexually and in every other way. ("AIDS is God's way of getting rid of the fucking queers, those filthy little perverts," he once told me.) He snorted and said I was "beyond the boondocks." So what? One can always drive to the ocean for stripping and swimming in sensual nakedness, cock and balls dangling free in warm salt water; snorkeling; tanning; or beach combing.

It must have been my second week, because I was in our little grocery store to replenish supplies, checking the shelf for packages of saimin, when a cart was pushed up to mine and a darkly resonant voice announced, "Hi, I'm Jim. You must be Bradley." I gave a swift glance, reluctantly. I admit this much: I was on my R and R and wanted to be left alone.

"Yes," I replied. I was noncommital, looking again for the shrimp-flavored oriental noodles.

"You've done proofing for Betsy Bane – on our local newsletter."

"Uh-huh." She was the editor, and her atrocious spelling was the bane of any proofreader's existence.

He was apparently not to be deterred. "So have I. She said I should meet you...that we have much in common."

"I've done some work for Betsy, when she catches and corners me."

He laughed understandingly. "Would you like to come to dinner?"

Such a mellifluous voice – all dark baritone lehua blossom honey. I finally really looked at him and involuntarily, openmouthed, took a quick breath: short of stature; thick black hair with a boyish cowlick; big and intense brown doe eyes, limpid, caressing, eyes to make one gasp; and a sensual ivory smile to dazzle (or break) your heart.

This is ridiculous, I thought. *Take off those rose-colored glasses. You're middle-aged, and he's getting there – a bit paunchy too.* I blinked, shook my head, and looked again to see the same incredible, impossible vision. I was abruptly tongue-tied, my mouth dry.

"I'm having five or six people this evening," he said. "Can you join us?"

"S-sure," I stammered.

I followed the directions to his Polynesian-style long house. The others were there already, six of them, all early. Everybody arrives too early out here – most inconsiderate – just when they're least wanted. Transplanted Californians. We call them coast haoles. I prefer the Pacific Northwest nomenclature: Californicators.

My host met me at the door and, as I kicked off my zori, I handed him a jug of chilled Portuguese white.

"Good stuff," he murmured approvingly.

When he took it from me, I let my hand slide down over his and couldn't stop myself from giving it a suggestion of a squeeze. I think, or I wanted to believe, it was returned.

Jim was the perfect host. He steered the conversation into the social and political banalities his other guests relished. He served drinks and caviar on toast points and a sumptuously creamy fresh mushroom-crab casserole with glass after glass of really good chablis. He followed the entrée, European style, with the salad, as I prefer. The others, albeit not overtly saying so, all too obviously didn't. I looked at Jim and saw that he was watching me. I winked. He covered a smile with his cloth napkin. We were already reading each other's minds.

The salad of locally grown greens and red onions, dressed with herbed olive oil and balsamic vinegar, was followed by a flawless flan. And then brandy — in warmed snifters, no less.

Some people, when wined and dined regally, never know when to go home. In deference to Jim I made the first move. At least they all took the hint. Shawls were retrieved and motions were made toward discarded shoes and slippers.

Aside, Jim gripped my elbow and said, *sotto voce* in those dark velvet tones, "Stay a bit." It was half a question, but from my grateful and — yes — lustful look, he knew it needed no answer.

We were now facing each other, at last alone, and he shrugged his shoulders as if in apology for the vacuous talk and the dullness of the company. I took a step closer, put a suddenly trembling hand gingerly on his shoulder, and stared into those entrancing doe eyes. "No need."

"Oh, yes, there is," he said. At first I didn't realize he had changed the subject. "I think we both feel a compelling need."

With that we were instantly embracing, holding, and squeezing each other as we hugged and kissed and roughly tongued and gave each other love bites and fumbled at our clothing.

Once naked, flesh to flesh, engorged cocks rigid, our throbbing and thrusting hard-ons pulsing with raging desire, we groped our way to his — our — bed.

We achieved orgasm after noisy orgasm, coming with and inside one another, orally, anally, each striving to become an inseparable part of the other. We cried out in joyous abandon, generating and spurting what seemed fountains of come, working each other up to ejaculation after massive ejaculation.

He was cut and loved fondling my foreskin with his fingers and lips. When he took me in his mouth, his lips eased my foreskin back and peeled it down below the head of my cock, exposing the glans and the sensitive nerve endings at its base. At the massage of his expert tongue, I cried aloud at the intensity of the pleasure.

Inevitably, reluctantly, our surfeited cocks softened, satiated, but still making spontaneous salutes, giving little involuntary jumps of joy, tender and chafed with whisker stubble. Our penis-spread sphincter muscles contracted hesitantly. Our nuts throbbed from being pumped out, damp ball sacs aching from being drained dry of what felt like every drop of their juices. The black hairs surrounding our nipples were still flattened and wet with saliva, and our still-erect nipples tingled, swollen and sore from sucking and pinching and nibbling. Our earlobes smarted from the harsh bites, and our lips felt bruised with rough endearments.

Ultimately, drowsily relaxed and entwined, we slept, exhausted, in a stupor of sexual ecstasy. "Stay a bit," he said. And I did — for ten delightful, delectable, delirious, and joyous years until brute cancerous death sought out my Ganymede and carried him off to a jealous Zeus.

THE TIME IS RIGHT

by Wayne J. MacPherson

The details surrounding the evening of January 10, 1973, are elusive. My destination was a meeting of Northwestern University Gay Liberation in Evanston, Illinois. I was a freshman and had come out only a month earlier, when — I swear — a lightbulb lit up over my head, cartoon-style, during my first kiss with another man.

In the intervening month I had fantasized about other men and about potential relationships. My ignorance about relationships did not interfere with my fantasies. In fact, it was the fantasies that made it an exciting time. But this January evening was reality. I was coming out in a group setting, my first big step in claiming a new identity. Even though it was the early 1970s and my college had a gay liberation group, I was still scared. If you had told me that I would be meeting the man who would be my partner twenty-two years later, I probably would have run away. Fortunately, I did not know and persevered.

I entered the student center, a relatively deserted and

foreboding concrete building, with my winter cap pulled down over my face. With a strange mixture of paranoia and self-aggrandizement, I was convinced I was being watched. Being sure I would confuse my followers, I went to the building's lower level even though I was destined for an upper floor. Eventually I found the meeting room. I entered it quickly and found a chair.

I cannot remember many details of that meeting — how many people were there, how long I stayed — but I do remember meeting a man that evening. A man glad to see a newcomer. A man wondering who the young man in disguise could possibly be.

I survived the meeting. Wisely I learned the man's name: Vincent McCoy. Vincent was rather infamous in campus circles. Since it was 1973, there were not a lot of black men proudly claiming their gay identity — at least, not on our campus. Being in a gay leadership position was difficult enough; being openly gay and black made you even more obvious. Thus, it was a mixture of physical attraction and attraction to his "fame" that intrigued me.

Most important, though, I learned a valuable lesson about first meetings: Second meetings cannot happen without them.

A week later I called Vincent, and we got together in his dorm room. It was late afternoon, and, if I recall correctly, I missed dinner that evening. I was young and newly out, but I was not slow. But it was the second meeting that counted. That meeting was the one where I noticed his smile. I remember how it illuminated his face and how it showed a mixture of openness and vulnerability. That smile is still there.

I remember thinking that our relationship was progressing too quickly. How could I have possibly met the man with whom I wanted to share my life only one month after coming out? Wasn't I too young — I had just turned nineteen — for such an event?

We forged ahead somehow. We spent many evenings together. We talked on the phone constantly. We still chuckle over the one evening we spent four hours on the phone — even making time for a break to hit the soda machine and the bathroom. We shared our common interests, including our common divas. I introduced him to Barbra Streisand's *Live at the Forum,* a recent Christmas present; he introduced me to *Color Me Barbra.* I introduced him to Liza Minnelli's *Liza With a Z* and to *Cabaret,* my favorite movie at the time. We shared the discovery of a new diva, though Vincent smugly remembers that I did not like Bette Midler at first. Appropriately or ironically, a Bette Midler concert that fall would be our first shared concert experience.

Fear set in, though, and we took a break from each other. Fortunately, during this separation, we had our only college class together, a lecture class called "Highlights of Astronomy." We spent most of the class periods trying to catch a glimpse of the other out of the corner of our eyes and looking away quickly when spotted.

After enough of this foolishness, we went back to his dorm room one day after class, fell on his bed, and I told Vincent I loved him. For the first time, I really meant what I said.

I will always remember Vincent saying something in those first months like, "Stop waiting for the white knight to appear on the horse and whisk you away." (Obviously, in our case, the image of whiteness was more than just an abstract metaphor.) He was telling me that relationships involve more than fantasy. They involve people who do not arrive according to an ideal timetable and who do not tailor themselves to fit a fantasy vision. All you can do is surrender to the timing and to the actual person who arrives.

After a long summer of separation and a year living together in a dormitory, we found our first apartment together, where we still live after all these years.

THE LONG GOOD-BYE

by Rich Petersen

It was late on the last night of an annual convention, and I was partying with other student personnel friends in Dallas. We had just finished a superb dinner at the Old Warsaw; much talk of mid-1970s college life — from the administrators' point of view.

Stu was there, of course. He was the main reason I went to all of those conventions and meetings. He and I had been having a fairly torrid affair for a couple of years, usually meeting at a convention (or in a couple of cases, inventing a convention to attend so our wives wouldn't suspect). Yeah, we were both married and both had two children — both boys. Stu was a lot more experienced at all this than I, though, as he had been having sex with men for a long time. But he was my first real affair, gay or otherwise, and I loved him for all he had shown me and for how nice he was about my naïveté.

But it was coming to a close. We were better friends than we would ever be lovers, and we both had families, neither

33

imagining how to deal with that aspect of our lives. So we agreed that those days in Dallas would be the start of another type of relationship for us.

"You have to go to the baths with me tonight," he said as we left the restaurant. "It's time you saw this." Stu was a "pro" at the baths and had gone often. It was the 1970s: no AIDS and lots of sex. I had never been to the baths before – never had the nerve – and was anxious for the experience. After saying our farewells to our friends, we set out across downtown Dallas. Stu walked everywhere, in this case through one of the seamier sides of Dallas, unbeknownst to us. Again, it was the '70s, 1976 to be exact, and there wasn't so much to fear then.

It was all so new…and nicer than I had imagined. Men everywhere, all kinds of men, all shapes and sizes. This cute guy at the desk asked me if I would do windows if we lived together…too much. Inside Stu took off after we said something about meeting up later. He knew what to do and where to go. I, on the other hand, knew nothing and so explored on my own. Very tremulous inside; no one to guide me. Orgy room too dark; I like to see. Then suddenly I was in the arms (and in the room) of a Cuban airline steward, getting fucked after my first hit of poppers.

As usual, I wanted to get to know this guy, but it was over very quickly and felt almost unreal because it was so fast. I showered and got dressed and went to the front lounge area to try to find Stu. I was really quite content but a bit tired. I thought about going back to my hotel, but there were so many men at the bathhouse, and I had already paid for the night.

Sex won as usual, and soon I was back wandering the halls in a towel. In the midst of watching a lot of action, I felt a hand under my towel feeling my cock and making it hard. Silky hair fell around my shoulders as this man kissed me and said, "Thank heavens I found you. I saw you as I came in." He must have looked into the lounge area where I had been sitting, but I didn't remember him at all. But now he was in charge, holding me so warmly, and I melted into him. His skin was the softest I had ever felt. No body hair, but he had marvelous long hair on his head that stroked me each time we moved.

Once we got to his room, we were naked in an instant and all over each other. I was amazed at how comfortable I felt; this wasn't like with the airline steward or with most anyone else I'd been with. The sex was slow and hot. When he went down on me, that silky hair brushed across my stomach and thighs and I thought I would die of pleasure. "What do you like to do?" I asked. "What you're doing now is just fine," he said as I pushed my cock into his mouth.

When we were through, neither of us made a move to leave. We talked and talked, our come-smeared towels draped over us. I learned that his name was Ernie. One of us said we should go out for coffee and food. It was 3:30 in the morning, and I was to fly home in a few hours to my wife and children, but I could do nothing but go with this man and spend the next few hours drinking coffee and smoking cigarettes, talking like I've never talked with any-one else before. He was so different, so special, and so won-derful. We held hands in one of Dallas's gay-friendly after-hours haunts. It was almost dawn, and we were still talking, asking each other any and all questions and answering with all honesty. We were so together in spirit and mind...but I was married. I had no idea what I could do to change that. There was nothing I could do. Ernie knew that.

Yet it was impossible to leave; we simply couldn't say good-bye. We parked near his apartment. We didn't go inside because he and his ex still shared space and they had agreed that neither would bring anyone else home. So we kissed and hugged and talked in his car. And cried. Yes, I remember we cried too, because we were so frustrated.

Finally, we agreed to get some sleep. He would pick me up at the hotel in a couple of hours, drive me around Dallas, and then to the airport. This way we would have more time together. Sleep – yeah, right. All I could do was pack and try to sleep, but I couldn't think of anything but this man I'd just met and how he had affected me, how I wanted to be with him. I was truly in love for the first time in my thirty-two years of life.

At 8:30 Ernie was at my hotel to pick me up. We went to a friend's place for breakfast, then to the airport. Ernie gave me a copy of *The Front Runner* to read. He had just finished it and wanted to share it with me now. Given my situation, it turned out to be a rather appropriate novel to read on my flight home, for what happened to us during the next four months has blossomed into a nineteen-year relationship.

We wrote and called almost every day and even managed to see each other a couple of times. By July it was impossible to maintain the charade of marriage any longer, and I left my wife and children and went to Dallas to live with Ernie. He was and is my best friend, and that is how it has felt since the beginning.

We feel this was meant to be, and obviously something is working after nineteen years. We have the same memory of that first night and retell it often.

As for my two sons, they are now in their mid twenties, and we recently saw one another after all these years. Following their mother's wishes, they hadn't seen or spoken to me in nineteen years. It was a wonderful reunion, though, and Ernie and I were accepted by them.

Makes me feel good, very good.

IN GOOD HANDS
by T.B.F.

At the end of summer, in the year after I finished high school, I left home and moved from Archdale, North Carolina, near Greensboro, to Charlotte. It was 1946. The war had ended, and there was little chance of my being drafted because Guilford County always had a surplus of volunteers to satisfy conscription needs for the armed services. I applied for a position with an interstate trucking firm that promised all-around automotive training and opportunities for advancement to drivers who signed on for at least a year. I wanted to get off the farm and see something more of the country than North Carolina's Piedmont had to offer.

At Southern Van Inc. I was taken on as an apprentice in motor maintenance. Our shop foreman's name was Jorg Johansen, but everyone called him JoJo. He was trained as a master machinist in the guild system in Norway in the late 1930s. When the Nazis took over his country early in 1940, JoJo stowed away on a Canadian freighter and came to the United States as a refugee to escape being drafted for munitions labor in a Nazi prison camp. When his special skills were discovered, he was recruited by Singer Sewing Machine in Bridgeport, Connecticut. During the war they had a government contract to make military small arms and build Sperry gyroscope mounts used for precision aerial bombing. JoJo stayed with Singer through the war, then drifted around and, for reasons unknown to me, wound up in Charlotte with Southern Van.

JoJo had been there about six months when I was hired. He ran a tight ship, kept his eye on everything that went on, and gave instructions with hands-on help. He was a private person — reserved but friendly — and almost never raised his voice. You took no offense when he corrected you because he did it, with authority, for your own good.

JoJo had wide, muscular shoulders and thick, hairy arms. He topped out at six foot two and probably was an exact copy of his Viking ancestors. His curly hair was cut short, so his head was crowned in ringlets the color of ripe grain. He was a rare sight in those days for having a trim full beard. Each morning JoJo would appear for work in a clean jumpsuit. By evening it would be streaked with grease from neck to knee — proof of his direct involvement in all the work turned out by his shop each day.

When I knew him, JoJo was about thirty years old. He was as sexy a hunk as I ever saw before or since. I couldn't look at him without getting hot. I'd get a hard-on every time he touched me, which happened now and then when he showed me how to handle tools.

During my first month at Southern Van, I was teamed up most of the time with a prissy apprentice named Willy. One day he told me he was going to quit, go back home to Siler City, and work in his daddy's garage. He also said, "Did you know JoJo has the hots for you?"

"You're crazy," I told him. "JoJo is straight. Anyway, he

doesn't know I exist."

"Nevertheless," Willy replied, "even though he may not know it himself, I know he wants to get inside your pants. I have a way of knowing, and I never make a mistake about things like that. I haven't made up my mind about you, though. Sometimes I think you're straight, but other times you come across as one of us."

"Do you go for men that way?" I asked him.

"I wish JoJo had a passion for me," Willy said. "I'd give anything to strip him naked, hold him close, and feel his dick go hard against me." Well, there was my answer. I threw a rod. My state of excitement would have been noticed by everyone in the shop had my Jockey shorts not been holding my cock tight against my belly and my baggy jumpsuit not hidden it from view.

From that time on I couldn't help feeling excitement whenever I was near JoJo. But he never gave any sign of awareness that I existed. Willy's fantasy of stripping JoJo quickly became mine. Many were the times I jacked off in my room thinking of him stroking my body and of me holding his dick. It was getting so that such thoughts were interfering with my work. JoJo had to criticize and correct me much of the time instead of giving me the brief praise for work well-done that I'd come to expect.

In my third month with Southern Van, everything suddenly changed. Bad luck hounded my steps all week. Nothing I did turned out right. It was near closing time on a Friday, and JoJo had just made me take a distributor head off three times before I finally set it straight. He stood waiting for me to finish, and I was humiliated by the ragging I'd taken from others. I barely heard the twang of heavy spring steel before I was rolling on the floor holding my shin and practically going blind from pain. A tire iron from the flat-change had sprung free, flown across the room, and, like a boomerang, hit me on the side of my right ankle. Pain blanched my face, and I thought I'd throw up. JoJo knelt to help me, but I just wanted to die. He told the others to go ahead and check out, he'd see that I got home. In about twenty minutes the pain let up enough for JoJo to move my foot and determine it was just a bad bruise. He asked me where I lived and whether I had anyone there to help until I was fit to care for myself. I shook my head and said, "If I can get home, I can make it. I'll be OK by morning." Then I gave him the address of my rooming house.

"I know the place," JoJo said. "Roomed there once. It's a crummy dump. You're coming to my place for the weekend. I'll look out for you until you can care for yourself." With that he picked me up as if my 145 pounds were no more than a sack of shavings and carried me out to his car. It was a black '36 Airstream Chrysler four-door sedan with fender wells and looked like it had just rolled off the assembly line. It purred like a Bentley and looked like it was doing sixty even when parked. All JoJo's love and skill showed in the care he gave his wheels.

By then I wasn't worried about my foot. The pain had died down to a dull ache, and my mind turned to thoughts of JoJo caring for me over the weekend. In two days almost anything can happen. Even if what Willy said wasn't true, JoJo might take a liking to me.

When we got to JoJo's place and parked, I tried to stand but blacked out the first time I put weight on my foot. I don't remember a thing until I awoke lying on the double bed in his apartment. He stood over me and said, "Rest here while I go to the pharmacy for crutches. You'll need them for a day or two at least."

His room served as a combination living room and bed-room with doors opening into a bath and kitchenette. Its furnishings were spare, but everything was neat and orderly — a far cry from the way I kept my place. A straight chair was in one corner, and an easy chair, floor lamp and bookcase were in another — but there was no couch, so I knew we'd be sharing a bed that night. The idea excited me. I felt heat in my crotch at thoughts of what might happen between us later.

Around eight o'clock he returned with crutches and a sack of hamburgers and fries. After eating, JoJo said, "We both need to clean up. You go first. Take a tub bath. You can't risk standing for a shower. I'll help you. I'll bathe later."

JoJo began drawing my bathwater as I removed my shoes, socks, and jumpsuit before hobbling into the bathroom on crutches. I was more concerned about flashing a hard-on than I was about any problems my foot might give me. The front of my Jockey shorts bulged out, and I hoped JoJo wouldn't notice my excitement. He steadied my back with one hand, pulled my shorts off with the other, then lifted me into the tub. With his hands on my naked skin, there was nothing I could do to keep my young manhood under control. There was no way he'd miss seeing the effect he had on me. I looked at his crotch to see if my excitement carried over to him, but his baggy fatigues hid everything happening inside. My face burned with embarrassment as my erection bounced and bucked while he gently soaped my foot and the rest of my body — everything, that is, except my privates. With a knowing smile he said, "I guess you can take care of *that* yourself." I grasped his suggestion, glad for a chance to hide evidence of my arousal with a washcloth.

JoJo left so that I could complete my bath alone, after which I drained the tub, then flooded it again with fresh water. I finished rinsing my body and was sitting in the tub drying off when JoJo knocked, looked in, and said, "I heard the water go down and thought you might need help." He lifted me to a sitting position on the john seat, knelt to finish drying my legs, and helped me put on a clean pair of his boxer shorts. He stood by to give help as I hobbled back to the bedroom.

My needs having been met, JoJo quickly undressed and returned to the bathroom. I had only a brief glimpse of his lanky body shimmering in a halo of blond hair as the bathroom door closed shut. The view was too brief for me to make a judgment as to whether he was well-hung or had just an average uncut dick on its way to getting hard. I'd never before been so stimulated. While awaiting his return, I turned down the covers, stripped off my boxers, and sat naked, waiting on the edge of the bed.

The sound of running water stopped, and a few minutes later JoJo reappeared, his naked body lit from the side in a way that emphasized his muscular development and mature maleness, which jutted out more than halfway to full erection. Only light from a streetlamp on the corner filtered into the room after JoJo switched off the bathroom light. Weight settled on his side of the bed. I was uncertain how to make what I wished for happen. We both were tense, uncertain, hopeful, and waiting for the other to make the first advance. JoJo broke the silence when he turned to ask, "Does your ankle hurt? Can I do anything for you?"

I faced him and said, "I'm OK. Thanks for everything." I felt the warmth of his body, and we began touching each other. Soon we were petting and holding dicks. It didn't take much of that for me to shoot hot spurts all over his belly, and that triggered the same response from him. All night and much of the next day we experimented, explored, held each other, made love, and enjoyed as wonderful a time as you'd ever imagine.

By Sunday we decided that I'd move in with him. In addition to the sex, which both of us thoroughly enjoyed, we got along well, with no friction or jealousy.

I was too young and sex-driven, however, to stop looking for other conquests. I continued my training under him for a while and then moved on to other on-the-job training. He was a private person who needed much time to himself, and he never talked freely about his past or his innermost thoughts. He knew me a lot better than I ever understood him. There never was a more completely male guy than JoJo; he was the greatest, my image of God's gift to mankind.

We separated amicably when he was offered a master mechanic position with a dealer in classic foreign cars in Pueblo, Colorado. The offer was too good to turn down both in pay and independence to work at exactly what he was trained for and most loved to do.

About six months after I got my driving papers, I arranged to get an assignment for a delivery of Tomasville furniture to an estate in Aspen, Colorado. I figured I'd run down and see JoJo on my return. By then he'd found a new live-in friend named Frenchie. I can't fault JoJo for that, but Frenchie was an unbelievably possessive, jealous, spiteful, and bitchy queen who hated my guts simply for knowing JoJo first and for having memories he couldn't erase. I had no cause to rock their boat, so I cleared out after inviting them to "come see me" if ever they were in North Carolina, but they never did.

Except for my wife, I never lived with anyone but JoJo for any appreciable block of time. She was a good woman, now gone to her rest, and fine mother to our three kids. I've no regrets there, but sexwise nothing in my life ever compared with what JoJo and I had going for a time. What a ride! The tenderness and heat of passion we shared were as good as such things can be for two people. No matter how brief it lasted, I'm forever grateful to have known that kind of happiness.

THE DAY WE MET

Although we were bunkmates and very close for the better part of a year, I don't recall our ever referring to ourselves as "lovers." Thinking back, I guess that's what we were.

HAPPY LANDING
by Eric Britten

I watched the horses disappear down the trail as the dudes and the guides headed out for their daylong ride. I raced through my chores as fast as I could. Chopped plenty of firewood to fuel the evening cookfire. Made sure the dinner meat was thawing. Filled the milk cans full of fresh spring water. Tidied up camp. Pulled the flaps down on all the tents in case of an afternoon shower. Pitched a tent for us a slight distance away from camp. Threw some clean clothes and a shaving kit into my gear bag. Jumped into my dented old Chevy half-ton. Jounced and bounced down the old logging roads to the KOA. Paid for a hot shower. Stripped out of my flannel shirt, boots, Levi's, Jockeys, and socks. Scrubbed myself under the steaming water, making sure I didn't miss the details: ears, neck, back, foreskin, asshole, crotch, between the toes. Toweled, dressed, spent an extra five minutes combing my hair and beard, slapped the dust off my XXXX beaver hat and checked the result. Hot fuckin' cowboy.

Gathered up my dirty clothes and toiletries. Stuffed them back into my duffel. Swung back through the office. Tossed a big grin and wave at Beth. Jumped down the steps to the parking lot. Tossed my gear into the truck bed. Climbed behind the wheel and spun out of the gravel drive onto the highway. Forty-two miles to Jackson. Only thirty-six to the airport.

Pushed the truck back down Highway 26 toward Moran. Turned south there. Twisted along above the Snake until it headed a bit west and the highway dropped onto the big flats. Clipped along as best I could, dodging the tourists and motor homes. Slowed. Turned right onto the airport road. Drove a bit more and parked a short way from the terminal building. Hiked across the lot and entered the building. Checked the arrivals. Ten minutes to spare.

I'd been rushing all morning. My only thoughts had been to get everything done so I could get to the airport before his plane arrived. Now that I had a few minutes to think, apprehension hit me pretty strong. Was I nuts, or did this make sense?

Three months ago my three female housemates had laughed at me when I decided to place an ad in *The Advocate's* personals section. I hadn't run into Mr. Right in the mountains of northwestern Wyoming and was running short of options. Repeated trips to Salt Lake City and Denver for vacations or long weekends hadn't yielded any boyfriends of substance. So it sure seemed like a reasonable alternative to me — sort of.

I leaned against the wall near the arrival gate and looked out the windows at the Tetons on the western horizon. He said he liked mountains, nature, and the wilds. Would he really? Santa Cruz, California, was a long way away geographically and philosophically from Jackson. Was he as down-to-earth as he sounded during the three telephone conversations we'd had over the past two months? Or was he one of those California slicksters just out for a good time at the expense of a mountain kid? Would he look as hot as he did in the photo he'd sent in his first of many letters? Was he as sincere about wanting to get away from the land of milk and honey as he said he was? Or would he taste a day or two of rural life and run back to the sunshine and easy life? Would he think I was as handsome as he said I was in my photo? Why couldn't I have sent him a better one? That self-portrait that I took in our kitchen using the timer on the camera wasn't exactly great.

I looked out and saw the small Frontier Airlines jet hit the runway. Small puffs of white smoke fumed from the landing gear as the wheels hit the tarmac. No time to worry now. I searched for a place to stand where I could watch the passengers file through the doorway. Not too close. I didn't want to seem too eager. Not too far away. I might miss him. But what if I didn't recognize him? What if he didn't recognize me? What would we do then?

The passengers began to come through the terminal entry. I searched each face for hints of the guy I was waiting for. Moms, dads, kids, an occasional pleasant-faced college kid, men, women — they slowly entered the terminal through the Jetway. I began to grow a little impatient. *What if he's missed the plane?* I remember thinking. *Naw. He'd have called ahead and left a message.*

Wait! There he was. Dressed in a polo shirt and Levi's. Carrying a day pack. His light brown hair was mussed from the long flight. Yup. That was him all right. He looked a lot like his photo. The mustache. The telltale tan. His green eyes searched the terminal for the face he hoped to recognize. Our eyes met. I shoved myself off the wall. His eyes brightened. Recognition flashed from them. I met his eyes and smiled. We slowly walked toward each other.

"Eric?"

"Rob?"

We stopped, facing each other. I almost wanted to hug him, but caution and prudence stopped me. I stuck out my hand instead. He grasped it firmly. Our eyes met again, moved over each other almost in unison and then rejoined each other. Grins flooded our faces.

"Wow," I managed to say. "You look just like you're supposed to."

He laughed. "You too." He sounded relieved.

Twelve years later, the same sparkle's in his eye. We still have those first photos. We still remember the first night together in that small green tent up in the Gros Ventre Range. He was the type of Californian my mother had warned me about. Thank heavens!

THREE'S A CROWD

by David Greig

Although it happened over thirteen years ago, the day I met my lover remains surprisingly clear in my memory. Other events in our lives since have dissolved into the ether of incremental forgetfulness, yet this one memory has stood the test of time — quite a feat, considering the roller-coaster ride our relationship has taken over the years.

It all started with a phone call. At the time, I was going through a promiscuous phase. Some of these trysts inevitably moved from enjoyable anonymous sex to annoyingly sticky entanglements. The caller — I always referred to him as David Bowie because his actual last name sounded like Bowie — was one such entanglement. After a few mediocre fucks, this person decided to try to cultivate a relationship with me. I was just not interested. But he was extremely persistent — so persistent, in fact, that he caused me to resort to the coward's dodge of refusing to answer my phone.

THE DAY WE MET

One Friday in early summer, I did actually answer the telephone. It was him. What was I doing that night? Visiting some friends. What about after? It would be very late. So? I would probably be drunk. He reminded me of my unusual physiological ability to keep a hard-on even when shit-faced drunk. After twenty minutes of the parry and thrust of excuse and cajole, he played a trump card. He told me he had set up a three-way. The guy was an architect, so we would be able to relate intellectually as well as physically. I hemmed. The architect lived in a fabulous apartment forty stories up, with a view of the whole city. I hawed. The guy had a beard. I relented. My friend — who was beardless — knew I was a sucker for men who, like me, had a beard. I told him that I would be there really late and really drunk. He gave me the address.

I spent the evening with friends, drinking and swimming in their pool. My curiosity about David Bowie's three-way got the better of me, however, and I left in time to catch the last call at a gay bar that was a few minutes' walk from the rendezvous site. After closing time, I casually sauntered over to the building where my friend and the bearded architect were presumably waiting. I still harbored suspicions that the third party may have been fictitious — or worse — but I rationalized that since the building I was heading toward was one into which the chronically unemployed David Bowie could not possibly have moved, then perhaps the person was real. With visions of twinkies and trolls dancing in my head, I rang the entry phone. David Bowie told me to come up.

I knocked, the door opened, and a man answered. I was hit with a bolt. I had read stories about love at first sight — about being struck by a sense of connection with someone who was a total stranger — but I thought such things were fictional romantic nonsense. Well, they're not. I have never felt such an immediate sensation of attraction to anyone before or since. What made the experience all the more incredible was that I could sense that the man on the other side of the door was feeling the same thing.

I entered the apartment and noticed my friend by the window. I sat down. The architect, Bill, was sitting directly across from me. We smoked a joint while David Bowie began to prattle on. I heard nothing. The only things I was aware of were Bill's eyes. They gazed into mine as we began a silent conversation of love and lust and conspiracy. Bill lifted his legs and placed them alongside me. I began to massage his legs and feet as naturally as if I had done this a thousand times before. We smiled at each other and began surrendering to the astonishing realization of the complete physical and personal ease that we felt with each other.

Suddenly, David Bowie got up and announced that after he returned from the washroom, we could all get down to it. Bill said the one thing that both of us were thinking: How can we get rid of my friend? I told Bill to go into another room and that I would rid us of the unexpectedly intrusive third party. Although I didn't even like David Bowie, I really didn't want to hurt his feelings. On the other hand, I knew that I had to get rid of him. Something was happening here with the man I had just met that I knew would turn into something more than just a one-night encounter. I somehow got the feeling that I had been looking for this man all along — a man I could really enjoy getting to know.

I told the host straight out that I thought I was falling in love with his friend and that even though it was cruel, I wondered if he could leave. In a calculated but understandable move, David Bowie said that he would not leave until I repeated to Bill why I wanted to be left alone. I felt no embarrassment as I told Bill that I thought I was falling in love with him. My friend surrendered and left.

THE DAY WE MET

Once the door was shut, Bill and I fell into each other's arms and stayed there for the next three days. In fact, we stayed there for the next thirteen years. Though we were ruthless with David Bowie, we have always been grateful to him as the person who — albeit unwittingly — brought us together. And although our once-electric lust has transformed over the years into more of a spiritually sustaining companionship, the memory of that first extraordinary evening has remained branded on my heart.

POTLUCK SURPRISE

by Peter House

When I was in high school, I had a mental picture of what my adult life would be like. I even envisioned the home I would live in: a cozy old house cluttered with books, some antiques, lots of plants, rocking chairs, and at least one cat. It would have a front porch to sit on, trees in the yard, and, in the summer, lots of flowers. It would be the kind of home people would feel comfortable in but not necessarily the kind that would impress anyone.

Not yet understanding myself in terms of sexual orientation, I pictured my wife and thought a lot about the kind of relationship we would have. She wouldn't be glamorous; she'd be attractive in a homey, comfortable kind of way. She would be warm, friendly, and perhaps a bit shy. She'd love cats, quiet evenings at home reading, and getting together with friends. For some reason I can't explain, I knew she'd wear glasses.

Our relationship would be secure, warm, and trusting. We'd laugh a lot together and be best friends as well as lovers. We wouldn't be Rhett Butler and Scarlett O'Hara; they were too passionate, too glamorous, too volatile. We'd be more like Norman and Ethel Thayer (Henry Fonda and Katharine Hepburn) in *On Golden Pond* — committed, stable, comfortable. That's not to say that we would have no passion and no romance; we would have the kind of passion and romance you could count on to last forever.

When I was in college, my values were challenged like they never had been before. I began to realize that my sexual orientation was leading me away from heterosexual marriage, and gradually the vision of my adult life that I'd had in high school disintegrated. What replaced it was mostly confusion and a sense of ambivalence about the future. The first few years that I was a part of the gay community, I could not even conceive of the idea that two persons of the same sex could maintain a long-term relationship of *any* sort, let alone a marriage like the one I fantasized about when I was sixteen. The gay "scene" seemed to be all about physical attraction and sex. Where were the long-term couples that could serve as my role models?

The relationships I had during this period (including one with a woman) all fell short of being even remotely like my fantasy marriage. Part of the problem was that I had lost this vision and didn't have a clear sense of what I wanted or needed from another person. Then, in the fall of 1987, I attended a pre-Thanksgiving potluck dinner sponsored by the gay and lesbian student group of the college where I was taking graduate courses. The event was held at the apartment of Tom and Dan, two students I had never met. I was instantly attracted to Tom. Unfortunately, I got the impression that he and Dan were lovers.

My friend Erik and I had brought two store-bought pumpkin pies and a can of Reddi-Wip. Tom remembers Erik and the pies, but he doesn't remember me. That's because he was busy playing host and I didn't really approach him, even though I wanted to. However, I vividly remember meeting him and thinking, *He's perfect for me. Why are all the good ones taken?*

I watched him — well, mooned over him, actually — all evening, wishing he were mine. The clearest picture I have of that night is of Tom sitting in the living-room armchair after the party had begun to wind down. He was holding one of his cats in his lap and affectionately petting and talking to her. I wished that I were sitting on the arm of the chair with my arm around Tom. I envied Dan, who, I thought, would be getting into bed with this great guy when the evening's clean-up was over, and I pictured them snuggling together and talking over the evening as couples do.

I was even taken with the apartment itself. It was a typical run-down, student apartment, but it had a certain homey coziness that's rare in these places. It felt like a permanent home and lacked the transient feeling that college apartments usually have. There were lots of books, plants, and cats around. And the kitchen was well-stocked, which suggested that someone did a lot of cooking. I wanted to move in on the spot.

But finally it was time to leave. I took one last wistful look at Tom and the cozy apartment, and Erik and I left.

Over the next year, I thought about Tom a lot. Sometimes I even went by his house hoping to catch a glimpse of him or sneak a peek at that cozy life through the windows.

When Tom and I met again at a party a year later, we talked for a long time and found that we had lots of mutual interests. I also found out that Dan was not his lover and that he was single! This was the first and only time I ever had the nerve to ask anyone out. And he accepted. Six months later I moved into that cozy apartment with him. Six and a half years and three cities later, we're still together.

GREEN LIGHT

Anonymous

Memorial Day weekend in Pensacola, Florida, has in recent years become a major drawing point for gay men from all over the United States. Crowds seem to grow exponentially each year. I have been vacationing there for about nine years now and never fail to have a total blast. But on May 28, 1992, the unexpected happened, changing the course of my own gay history forever.

I was taking a drive quite late at night along the beach highway fronting the Gulf of Mexico. There was little traffic, and I was relieved to temporarily escape the rush of people visiting the city for the holiday weekend. As I ended my little excursion and returned to the city, I pulled up at a red light. I looked over rather absently at the car in the turn lane next to mine. Something popped in my head. The guy in the other car was about as plain and nondescript as one could imagine — early twenties, glasses, really short mousy brown hair. Yet something in our eye contact established an almost cosmic force, a bond that has lasted to this very day.

Our eyes connected for not more than five seconds. Then the light turned green, and I slowly inched forward. I noticed in my rearview mirror that, rather than turning left as he intended, he had pulled over into my lane. I continued along, actually only half aware that a game of cat and mouse was under way.

At the next signal he pulled up alongside me and looked at me again. This time our eyes connected for perhaps ten seconds. On the green light I continued gaily forward but soon made an abrupt right turn onto a side street. Damn! It was a dead end. I was trapped. I attempted to back up and turn around; he was right behind me and began to maneuver his vehicle as well. I pulled up right next to his car. Normally a very shy person, I just knew I had to speak to him. I rolled down my window and said (quite brazenly for me), "Well, hello, sailor."

He showed me the most incredible smile I have *ever* seen. He asked me what I was up to, and some innocuous chitchat commenced. After about five minutes we decided to move over a few blocks to a city park, where we could sit and talk under the stars.

I must point out that I was not really looking for anyone that night, nor was I in a particularly horny mood. Yet with each passing moment in our conversation, I became more and more intrigued by his presence. What started out as a cordial, everyday-type chat grew over the next three or so hours into a feeling of warmth, release, relaxation, and almost total trust. We bared our very souls, sharing our childhoods, our dreams, and our hopes...until eventually we saw the beginnings of sunrise and a new day.

I invited him to breakfast. After our meal we spent the rest of the day and most of the next evening in my hotel room. And the one thing that let me know I had finally met Mr. Right was that relatively *little* of our time together was spent having sex. Mostly we talked and talked and talked...and just held each other.

He lived in Nashville at the time; I was working in the Atlanta area. Over the next few weeks, we visited each other frequently, Nashville and Atlanta being only a few hours apart by interstate. By mid July he moved down to Atlanta and we started our new life together. We now reside in Florida, and as I write this, we are about to celebrate our third anniversary. This past Memorial Day weekend, we revisited the "scene of the crime" – the intersection where we met and the park where we chatted – and even stayed in the same hotel and the same room in which we spent our first day together.

To this day I contemplate all that never would have happened had he decided to turn left at that traffic signal in downtown Pensacola.

THE CLUB PUPPY

by Christopher Paw

I waited on the ratty and frayed sofa in the putrid brown reception area, my hands sweating, and rehearsed what I wanted to say. I wasn't certain I was ready to jump headlong into the AIDS field of my industry, but was disenchanted and disappointed with the fund-raising I was doing with one of the big five disease societies.

The volunteer receptionist, an aging club puppy who had deluded himself into believing he could still wear short shorts, cropped hair, and attitude underlined the fact that I wasn't exactly in the corporate world. Seeing that I was nervous, he started in with the small talk. Another indication that I was in a service-based industry instead of a money-raising one. I feigned interest in what he was saying but wondered how I could possibly raise a half million dollars with a receptionist who dressed like Cindy Lauper.

I got the job.

I was now an employee of the city's largest AIDS organization, where screaming queens, addict transvestites, and confrontational bull dykes roamed. I learned quickly not to gawk, though not as quickly as I learned to book corporate sponsorship meetings on neutral territory.

In the crowded smoking room in the back of the office, I was beginning to fit in. There was the odd philosophical disagreement with counselors and education staff. But my being HIV-positive at least gave some weight to my more conservative outlook.

I was bonding with the volunteer coordinator, a lipstick lesbian named Betty-Ann, when the receptionist bounced into the smoke-filled room. He kissed Betty-Ann and plunked himself on the chair beside me.

"Congratulations on the job," he said, smiling and lighting a cigarette.

Great, I thought, *the club puppy.* "Thanks," I replied. I wrinkled my nose and raised my eyebrows. Betty-Ann understood and responded.

"Chris, this is David, or Daszy. Daszy's a longtime volunteer. He does a little bit of everything, but right now we've got him working reception."

"Oh, nice to meet you," I offered.

He kissed my cheek. "Welcome. It's good to have a new face around." He squeezed my thigh and winked. My muscles tightened as I wondered how I was going to get out of this tiny room without offending anyone. Then someone poked his head in the door.

"David, line one's for you."

He jumped out the door. "See you later, sweetie."

Regaining my composure, I leaned back in my chair and relaxed my shoulders a little. "He's a live one."

Betty-Ann laughed. "Yeah, but he's great. And he thinks you're hot."

That was *not* what I wanted to hear. It was obvious that Betty-Ann and this Daszy person were good friends. She was the first person in the office I felt I could maintain a conversation with, and now she was connected with this ditzy freak who wanted me. Maybe the corporate world wasn't so bad after all.

That day as I slid my in/out marker to the out position, Daszy handed me a slip of paper.

"Call me sometime."

I nodded. "Yeah, sure." And ran out the building.

For two weeks Daszy the receptionist dogged me. He watched the hallway for when I went for a smoke and conveniently took his break at the same time. He found out what coffee shop I went to in the morning and was always sitting there when I arrived, bleary-eyed, for my first caffeine infusion of the day. He brought lunch to my desk when it became apparent that I was having a busy day and wouldn't get out. He delivered my messages by hand and gave my calls priority when he was answering the phones.

In reception, after the conclusion of a volunteer meeting, Betty-Ann nabbed me as Daszy pranced through.

"What do you think of him?" she asked.

"He's nice enough," I replied. "I guess he's cute. Just not my type."

She smiled. "He really likes you. Wouldn't it be great if you got a lover along with the new job?"

I winced a smile. "Yeah, wouldn't it."

That night, I finally realized that this man was obsessed. I reasoned that since I had to work with him, I had to do something about the situation. So I pulled out the crumpled paper with his number and called. We made a date for dinner Friday night.

I figured if I were the most obnoxious person I could be during dinner, I could completely turn him off and be rid of this nuisance. It was a proven plan that had worked in the past.

Friday night came, and I rang the buzzer to his apartment building. When I got to his door, he greeted me followed by his cocker spaniel. "I'm glad you came."

Daszy was subdued, controlled, and reasonable throughout the predinner conversation. He was even wearing the standard fagwear of a T-shirt and jeans. I had trouble being the intolerant asshole I had planned to be. When he served a candlelit dinner on his balcony in the warmth of late spring, suddenly the city disappeared.

Outside the office David was no longer overbearing. His flamboyance faded as his sincerity cracked the surface of his facade. There was a sparkle of mischievous charm in his eyes. As the evening wore on and the wine mellowed my pretentious attitude, I truly relaxed for the first time in months. This time I didn't flinch when he put his hand on my thigh.

I left Sunday afternoon.

Monday *and* Tuesday mornings I arrived at work to find a dozen red and white roses on my desk. Daszy was back over the top. It is still his most annoying quality, though it can be very flattering. At first I wasn't certain whether I wanted the whole adventure to be a one-night stand. But David has a way of maneuvering himself to the place where he wants to be.

We kept dating. And with standard fag cautiousness with regard to relationships, I moved in with him three months later. He had a tiny bachelor apartment, which we shared with his ailing cocker spaniel, my aging cat, and two cockatiels. But it was close to work...

...where I was starting to hear tales of our sex life in the crowded smoking room. David was so proud to have snagged me despite my hesitations that he bragged like a sixteen-year-old.

David still cooks dinner for me almost every night. In four years I've discovered his culinary repertoire to be much grander than the simple pasta he presented on our first dinner date. Now in our third apartment, we've adopted another cocker spaniel as his didn't make it through our first year together. My cat is still hanging on, though we've traded in the birds for a rather large fish tank. They're quieter.

All of this wraps up to sound like a romantic fairy tale, but it just ain't so. We argue frequently, as most couples do, but our arguments are tainted with the personal fear of losing each other — not to some other man or to a better job in a different city, but truly losing each other. As the years have gone by, we've watched our prescription-drug orders rise while our personal strength drains. The love is very real, but so is the fear.

But we're still learning to enjoy every moment we have even in the midst of a misdirected argument. And he doesn't wear those ridiculous trendy outfits anymore, except on pride day. I can live with that.

THE WAITING GAME
by Alan Irgang

G rant and I have been together for over two years
now. Is this a long-term relationship? Well, for *me* it
certainly is. Oh, I know there are no guarantees that
anything lasts forever, but I *do* know that he is the only man
I have ever met that I feel I could spend the rest of my life
with.

We met on a blind date. I remember it so well. We were
set up by mutual friends who had been a couple for a year.
They thought we might hit it off. On Grant's suggestion we
met at a restaurant in "Boys' Town" on the north side of
Chicago. It was a rather upscale place, which suggested to
me that he had class. But pretentiousness really turns me off,
so I was mindful to watch for possible clues.

I arrived my usual ten minutes late to find him waiting at
the bar. I had been thinking (but not obsessing) about this
date all week, wondering if he'd be cute, conversational,
intelligent, and witty. I had learned over the years what I like
in a man. I was delighted to learn that he was all of this and

so much more. Was it love at first sight? Definitely not. I had learned the hard way that first-date fireworks mean only one thing — turn and run the other way as fast as you can and don't look back! All those relationships that started out with intense enamor never lasted and usually left me with nothing but heartache. No, this time I would do it differently. I decidedly set out to let this evolve and not to *create* a relationship. If it worked out, great. If not, I still have *my* life. I had contributed enough to my therapist's retirement fund by this time to have learned to be content by myself without being attached at the hip like Velcro to another love-starved man.

Anyway, back to that first date. After we were seated I had to resist the temptation to bury my face in the menu to avoid those first awkward moments. Yeah, it felt uncomfortable, but not like previous first dates. I didn't feel as if I had as much riding on this one. I used to get so disappointed when the first date didn't work out. That's a real setup for failure, so I learned to go into dating situations without any expectations. This leaves no room for disappointment.

I also had to resist the temptation to drill him with my repertoire of fifty questions, starting with, "So tell me about your mother." I used to do that until I learned that the brighter guys caught on and responded with what they figured I wanted to hear. I was snowed many times. Instead I treated him like a friend and not like a candidate on *The Dating Game.* The conversation was well-balanced. I talked about myself, he talked about himself, and we had a great meal together. He was warm and charming with a great sense of humor and a peacefulness I had rarely experienced before. I liked him.

Did I ever once during that meal wonder what he looked like naked? You bet I did. What homosexual man with a fantastically erotic imagination wouldn't? In the past I would have found out before the end of the night. But another rule I had established after many unsuccessful relationships was no sex for three months. Why three months? I don't know, it just seemed like a good period of time to get to know someone before making decisions about sex. Actually, it had never really been a decision before. It's just what we do, right? The big question was usually whether we should cook breakfast or eat out. However, in the past I hadn't allowed myself to really get to know the guy first. So when the sex became dull, it was over. There was nothing else to sustain the relationship.

We had a really nice time. After we left the restaurant, I offered to give him a ride home. He declined at first but then accepted my offer. I didn't realize at the time that he lived just three blocks away. When we got to his place, we exchanged the obligatory cordialities and said good-bye. There was no kiss.

Months later he revealed to me that he had wanted to sleep with me that night and was insulted that we didn't even kiss. I really played up the prude bit. But my determination to avoid just one more hot and steamy encounter laid the foundation for the next three months of anticipation. And it was well worth the wait. We "consummated" our romance on New Year's Eve in a ritzy hotel room. Yes, it was *the* most romantic evening of my life.

For our first anniversary we went back to that restaurant and reenacted our first date. I arrived my usual ten minutes late and we had some great fun. The waiters were quite amused as well; We were very convincing.

In a few months Grant and I will be moving in together. Our love for each other has continued to flourish and mature. The casual pace at which our relationship developed is the key to our success. We have the utmost mutual respect and trust and, most important, unconditional love for each other. I cherish that first night we met as it was the seed that with loving nurturing, patience, and tenderness has evolved into the most gratifying relationship of my life.

THE MELODY OF THE MOON
by John David Dupree

C an it really be nearly twenty years since I decided to take off my black lace veil and declare the end of my thirteen-month mourning period? After the heavy drama of "Omigod, my first Easter/gay pride parade/Fourth of July/Labor Day/Halloween/birthday/Thanksgiving/ Christmas/New Year's Eve/Valentine's Day without Glen," launching into another round of "Omigod, my second Easter, etc. without Glen" even threatened to make *me* yawn.

Now, I'm generally not one to get bored with my own melo-drama, you understand. But my friends were starting to avoid me, with such likely excuses as, "Well, I need to run and buy a tarp to cover the garden so the rain doesn't hurt the rhubarb." Since I'd become the only truly devoted audience member still obsessed with my plight, I figured the cosmic message might be that it was time to put the past behind me and beat the bushes for a man with whom to share my life.

Ruling out a life in the monastery, however, which way was I to go? I met my wife of ten years, an auburn-haired

WASP, on the job, when were both working for a newspaper in Michigan. I met the first man of my life – a Jewish South African – at the Berkeley Men's Center during the ninth year of my marriage. Eight of the ten years with my wife had been mutually monogamous, and for most of the six years with him I had been faithful, though I was never led to believe it was mutual.

Should I start looking at my workplace, where most of the employees were lesbians or gay men? Should I make another pilgrimage to the Men's Center and hope to repeat my good fortune of nearly seven years earlier? Since I'd never tasted anything alcoholic and couldn't stand the smell of smoke, bars were not a viable option. I've never had any desire to go to the baths, the parks, or "adult" bookstores with "active" back rooms, since anonymous sex and long-term relationships seemed somehow mutually exclusive.

I tried the Pacific Center's gay men's rap groups, but the issues most of the guys were dealing with (e.g., coming out to Mom and Dad or on the job) I had dealt with so long ago that it was a bit like driving with my eyes glued to the rearview mirror rather than watching the road ahead. And besides I was already working thirty hours a week at the Pacific Center as a "professional faggot," so this wasn't exactly a stimulating change of scenery for me.

As it was the 1970s a revolutionary new phenomenon was emerging in the gay centers of the world. Much like the *San Francisco Chronicle* devoted its pink pages each week to the arts, *The Advocate* began enclosing a pink section also, but largely devoted to men on the prowl who had perhaps exhausted all other avenues for meeting Prince Charming. But wasn't this a risky thing to do? A good way to get one's throat slit or one's belongings stolen? Wasn't meeting someone through a classified ad tantamount to asking for trouble? Sure, it's an OK place to locate a used car, a different career, or a new apartment, but a relationship…?

I experimented with every other format imaginable (e.g., fearfully agreeing to give my phone number to a man carrying a bag of peat moss outside the hardware store, having an affair with a lesbian in a political action group fighting an antigay referendum). I finally decided that I might *respond* to an ad but that I'd certainly never run one. That would be a sign of real desperation.

The ads that I responded to over the next six weeks resulted in everything from dullness and slight sweetness to horror. Having someone tell you on the first date that he really likes thrusting into a guy bent over in the shower is not my idea of a first-date kind of conversation. Whatever happened to courtship rituals? Nearly as off-putting, however, was hearing on the first date about the fifteen things a loan officer considers when dealing with a mortgage application. This was especially hard to hear from someone who, as it turned out, was still married and not out to his wife, family, or coworkers. We could be "secret lovers" on Tuesdays between 4 and 6 p.m. and the occasional Saturday morning, when his wife expected him to be processing loan applications. Who could pass up a deal like that?

I had just about given up hope — figuring I'd either wind up committing suicide like they did in the great lesbian novels of the fifties or growing old lonely, rejected, and despised by family and society alike — when I noticed this ad: BLACK GAY MAN, 34, LOOKING FOR LONG-TERM RELATIONSHIP WITH WHITE GAY MAN, UNATTACHED, WANTED TO SHARE LIFE. I thought it was a direct, just-sharing-enough-to-be-interesting kind of ad, minus the usual gory details about fetishes, cock size, and propensity for chats by the fire.

Though I'd had many friendships with black men over the years, none of those relationships had culminated in a very intense emotional, much less sexual, way. Having been involved heavily in the black civil rights movement over the years, I had always maintained the politically correct posture that I would be open to a more in-depth relationship with black, Hispanic, Asian, or Native American people. But I'd never really done anything about it. Maybe this was the time to call my own bluff, I told myself, taking a deep breath and sitting down at my newly purchased IBM Selectric.

Jumaane responded to my heartfelt but cautious letter (no mention of fetishes, cock size, or fireside chats but definite allusions to playing music together, the role of my two kids in my life, plus the urge to travel). When he called me back a couple of days later, the conversation was a bit strained, but we agreed that we would meet on the weekend. We arranged that he would come to my house. After all, I knew that *I* wasn't an ax murderer, so it was safe for him to come to *my* house, but I didn't know about *him*, so...

On the appointed Saturday afternoon, I changed clothes three times, beginning to harbor doubts about letting a strange man into my house. I compromised on the bumpkin-clone look — blue jeans, red plaid shirt, and rainbow suspenders, which wasn't too sexy (like cutoffs and a tank top would be) or too frumpy (like my bib overalls might have been). As 4 o'clock rolled around and I had resolved to follow through with the meeting, I started looking out the window for a glimpse of the guy before he came to the door.

At exactly 4 o'clock, I saw a large Dodge pickup truck with matching camper shell pull up outside. A black man got out, glanced at a piece of paper in his hand, looked at the house number, and started across the street. My heart skipped beat or six, my life flashed in front of me, and then I finally took a second to notice what the guy really looked like. He looked like a regular guy, kind of nervous, apparently well-put-together under his khaki windbreaker and matching military-type khaki pants. He was something of a Lionel Richie look-alike, minus the mustache.

Since getting to my door involved coming up the side of the house and through a big wooden gate into the backyard, my would-be friend disappeared from sight for a few minutes. *Maybe he's changed his mind,* I ambivalently feared and hoped. When the knock finally came at the door, not wanting to appear too eager, I counted to ten like my old football coach used to — one thousand one, one thousand two… — made sure the suspenders weren't pulling my jeans up too snug, took a deep breath, and answered the door.

Describing the next ten minutes as awkward seems a bit of an understatement, since neither of us had ever done anything quite like this before. Luckily, we both grew up Methodist (he African Methodist Episcopal and I United Methodist) and had played the piano and organ for our respective churches in our youth. So we glommed on to that link like drowning men clinging to a floating two-by-four. Each of us took turns playing my little rental spinet, initially plinking pieces from the Methodist hymnal, then working into classical, pop, show tunes and Scott Joplin rags.

Music in general, and the piano specifically, has always been one of the most effective tools for dealing with stress in my life. Having worked in high-pressure jobs since my teens, I know that I can alter my mood by sitting at the piano. If I'm terribly depressed at the end of the day, playing the piano can buoy my spirits to a point where I'm actually a pretty pleasant and outgoing person. Similarly, if I come home totally wired, I can tickle the ivories for a few minutes and shift gears down to a point where I'm no longer fuming, anxious, or a borderline sociopath.

In this getting-to-know-you stage of the relationship between Jumaane and me, the piano played that same facilitating role. While each of us listened to the other play, we at first only pretended to be casual and relaxed with another. But by the time we were tapping our feet together to *Maple Leaf Rag* or harmonizing to *One Hand, One Heart* (he's a tenor, I'm a bass), we were becoming genuine friends. Because of this natural flow during our first afternoon together, it felt like the truth for a few years when I indulged my initial embarrassment about our pink-pages meeting by saying, "Oh, we met at a party at my house!" It had become a party, I rationalized. How many in your party, sir? Two.

Since Jumaane was considerably more experienced than I was, our ideas of how the evening would end were quite different. I had been sexual with two women and three men my entire thirty-five years on the planet. Jumaane shared early on that he'd been in bed with five priests *at the same time* a few years back.

Those of us considered to be prudes by many experienced folks are a highly misunderstood segment of society. It's not that I didn't notice or get turned-on by the firm-looking buns in the back of his khakis, the bulges in the front, or the smooth chest peeking out of the open collar of his shirt. As much as I fantasized about touching, smelling, and tasting every square (and round) centimeter of this newfound hunk, the first order of business for me was to know this young man as my friend, someone who could be trusted to be a friend for life. It's not worth it to me to be sexual with anybody who doesn't meet that need. I would rather masturbate than have sex with someone I didn't trust completely.

At the end of that first evening, we agreed we both wanted to spend more time together. Music and dance became the focus for the evolution of our friendship over the next few weeks. Returning to my house in Berkeley after seeing the San Francisco Ballet present a very erotic production of choreography, Jumaane and I adjourned to the upstairs bedroom, the full moon shining down on the bed through the skylight, and the party of two became a party of one.

A few weeks after this all-night consummation, we made a contract that, in retrospect, may have saved one or both of our lives. We agreed that our relationship would be an open one, that each of us could be involved with other people as long as there were no secrets. But there were explicit rules attached to that openness. Oral, anal, or vaginal sex, reported to facilitate sexually transmitted diseases, would be forbidden outside the relationship. Only nonpenetrative sexual practices would be allowed with others. In the eighties the importance of that safe-sex contract became obvious.

And now, nearly two decades later, having raised three children, lived on two continents, and faced umpteen crises together, neither of us has major regrets over our musical, sexual, or general friendship connections. If things ever seem a bit rocky between us, I can sit at the piano, play the introduction to Dionne Warwick's *That's What Friends Are For,* and know that Jumaane and his mellow tenor will soon be there beside me on the piano bench. We continue building our life together based on the sound foundation laid in the seventies, and, as often as possible, we commemorate the full moon.

GETTING COZY

by Barry Zeve

Larry and I met when we were both thirty-seven years old. My age was important to me because I had dreamed of meeting a special partner since I was twelve years old. I had pushed to make it happen, but it never had. By my mid thirties I felt that life had forgotten me, that I would never experience the joy of intimacy between lovers. By the time I met Larry, I had already stopped pushing. I figured if it was meant to be, it would just happen. I stopped hoping "he" would turn up behind every corner. I had always left room in my life for a lover, but I had never set aside enough room in my life for me. *Love the one you're with,* I told myself. So I sought the courage to live in peace with myself.

My inner voice told me to leave the city and move to the country. I quit my job as a junior high school teacher in East L.A. and moved to a small town of nine thousand people in the wine country of Northern California. I had never lived in a farming town. I had never had a pet. I had never witnessed the changing of the four seasons. This was, as my father used to say, "A chance to kill a never."

Following my dream of living in the country did not mean that I gave up my dream of finding Mr. Right. It just superseded it. It meant putting myself first.

I was always attracted to foreign men, the sort of man I was more likely to meet in L.A. or another big city. I had always hoped to be partnered with an exotic man, someone who spoke with a foreign accent, someone whose skin, hair, and eyes spoke of lands I had only visited or hoped to visit. When I met Larry I was attracted to his olive skin and large, dramatic, organ-grinder style mustache. But I was disappointed when I found out that he was Jewish, like me. I didn't think that made him exotic at all. I tried not to be prejudiced, least of all against someone from my own culture, but I admit that some of the ideals I was looking for in a man had to be discarded. Later I was very happy to discover just how much Larry and I had in common culturally.

We met at a gay men's spiritual retreat on February 16, 1990, two days after Valentine's Day. The retreat was in a secluded part of the redwood forests along the Russian River. There were about twenty-five men, all strangers to me, who met for a three-day weekend in a beautiful Victorian mansion.

The best part of being in seclusion with all those gay men was the opportunity to watch Larry as he socialized with them. There were so many questions I didn't have to ask him; his behavior in public spoke for him. Although we spent time alone, the time we spent sharing community told me a lot about him. I remember in high school watching the boys and the girls socialize freely together. I missed it then. I watched Larry carefully that weekend. I noticed whom he spoke to, what he laughed at, what he ate and drank. I learned a lot about him indirectly.

The second night of the weekend, the group got together in a circle. Each person was instructed to give himself a Native American name. My heart sank. I hate doing things like that. I looked back at the door, but I didn't see a graceful way out of the room. I know I would have been just as uncomfortable if the assignment had been for each of us to give himself a Hasidic name. I felt that they were toying with another people's culture.

When it was Larry's turn to give himself an Indian name, he just turned to the group and said, "I'm Larry Wisch, Urban Dweller." Everybody laughed, and I think I fell in love with him on the spot. I saw he had a sense of humor and that he could use it to get himself out of an uncomfortable situation. Larry never met a stranger. He's curious; he asks questions, a rare virtue in most social circles. He will talk to anybody without seeming to worry about being judged; he's too busy enjoying being himself.

Larry found me attractive in part because of how I was carrying myself through a problem I was having at that time. I had found a job teaching in a rural junior high school, but my students started to suspect that I was gay and began to taunt me. Rather than hide my sexuality or lie, I decided to come out to my students. The administration, teachers, and parents rose to the "threat" overnight. Parents pulled their children out of my classes, teachers stopped talking to me in the lunchroom, and the administration started to "monitor" my classes in an effort to find reasons not to hire me the following year. Larry admired me for the way in which I walked through that challenge. He found me attractive, not just good-looking.

We didn't sleep together on the first night. That waited until the second night. I was staying in a cabin outside the main house, and it was so cold that I couldn't sleep at all the first night. So Larry invited me to sleep with him on his twin-size bed. I was warm, but we were chaperoned the whole night by his roommate, so the climate was close but not intimate.

We got to know each other better and better over the next few months and realized that we wanted to be soul mates — to share some things, to divide others. We wanted to witness the integrity and love of each other's spiritual path, to forgive and accept in each other's presence. We didn't meet a moment too soon or too late. If we had met thirty-seven years later, it would be just as sweet.

A CAPITAL AFFAIR

by Steven Riel

Neil and I first met in the fall of 1980 at a reading I gave at the Gay Community Center in Washington, D.C. I was in my senior year at Georgetown University. The reading was a very big deal to me at the time. People whom I admired and wanted to impress were there: my favorite professor attended as well as a few of my mentors on the staff of Georgetown's literary magazine. Several friends were also there, and I had invited everyone to a party at my apartment afterward.

Following the reading, strangers came up and critiqued my writing and presentation. This was still a new experience for me. Neil came up with another man and introduced himself, offering some good criticism of the short story I had read. He said he was writing a novel and wanted to get together to talk about writing. We exchanged phone numbers, and, feeling awkward, I joked about the sexual implications of doing this. I assumed that the other man, Bob, was Neil's lover.

My first meeting with Neil did not stand out in my mind, because of Bob's presence, I suppose, but also because so many other things were going on that evening. I was worried about so many different things: I hadn't bought the avocados early enough for them to be soft for the party; the guests from different parts of my life wouldn't hit it off; a few weeks earlier, my roommate had told me that he wanted to have a romantic relationship with me, and I was trying to say no to him gracefully while still living together (and having a party for my friends at our apartment); there was someone else coming to the party whom *I* had a minor crush on; and I had a raw patch of skin on my penis that had me scared.

Not too many days afterward, Neil called me. His Long Island accent seemed much thicker on the phone. I remember these first phone calls as being clumsy and tentative. We made plans to go out a few weeks later on a Saturday night, postponing our first date until a week after I was scheduled to take the Graduate Record Examination. I had a part-time job at a run-down bookstore located a few blocks south of Dupont Circle, so Neil would pick me up there after work.

There was no bathroom in the bookstore, but I had a key to an internal door to the office building next door and could use the bathroom there. Nervous before my date, I locked the front door of the store a minute or two before closing time and rushed to the bathroom to primp (and to arrange my genitals to their best advantage inside my pants). When I headed back to the store, the door between it and the office building lobby was locked shut. A draft must have pushed or pulled the door closed, and it locked automatically. I went to the front of the lobby and saw Neil outside the bookstore. I knocked on the window, and he approached. I shouted an explanation through the window. I was extremely embarrassed, but Neil later said that, ironically, this was a good start because the comedy inherent in the situation broke the ice. I asked Neil to go call Zac, the store's owner. While we waited for Zac to arrive with a key, Neil and I made faces through the glass and shouted to one another.

Once I was liberated, we walked up to Trio's, a very inexpensive diner-style restaurant heavily patronized by gay men. Inside it was like a scene from *Laverne & Shirley:* The waitresses were middle-aged; had dyed, bouffant-style hairdos; brusquely slid our plates onto the small table; and called us "sweetheart." The food was middle-American and one or two steps above that found in TV dinners: chopped sirloin, roast chicken — everything served with a thick gravy. Each of us admitted we felt more comfortable at a place like this than at a chichi café.

I was immediately attracted to Neil. He was tall, muscular, hirsute, and had warm, brown eyes. His clothes were more hippielike than we wore at Georgetown, but I was intrigued by that difference. (At that time, it was terribly cool to look preppy, partly in revolt against the way-out clothes of the sixties. Even my classmates who had gone to public school dressed in topsiders, chinos, and Lacoste shirts).

I was impressed that Neil not only knew of the philosopher Herbert Marcuse but also had majored in European intellectual history at Cornell. He had written his thesis on Marx and Freud. Georgetown's curriculum was by and large conservative. There was only one course that focused on leftist political ideas. I had taken it in the spring, before I met Neil, and Marxist theory had stood many of my earlier assumptions upside down.

Neil was four years older than I and had had several interesting experiences since his graduation. He had been involved in a Marxist-feminist organization and had traveled to Europe, visiting some of the group's members there. He had worked at a mental hospital and had taught nursery school. He was working at Gallaudet University and studying American Sign Language there. I felt somewhat provincial and inexperienced by comparison.

In a skillfully oblique way, he maneuvered the conversation to a discussion of tricking and committed relationships between men, and we both admitted that we didn't like going to bars and tricking. Neil said that he preferred to stay home and read but that he was so tired when he got home from work at night, reading often put him to sleep, so he'd end up going out instead.

After we had finished eating, I didn't want the evening to end, so I invited him over to my apartment to listen to music. Neil wanted to show me how he could sign a song or two in sign language. I hadn't thought about the possibility that my roommate might be home, and, sure enough, he was. He glared at us — it was horrible, because I knew what he was feeling. I showed Neil some of the literary magazines my writing had been published in as well as some of my photo albums. He signed Bette Midler's song "The Rose" for me. That had been the song my previous lover and I considered ours. I thought about my ex a lot that night while I was looking at Neil.

Neil suggested that we go to out to hear a singer. We talked more about writing (and about sex!) and stayed for two sets of songs. Afterward we hugged — somewhat nervously, I thought — in the middle of Dupont Circle, and each headed in a different direction home. As I walked east down Massachusetts Avenue, past all the embassies, I wondered what Neil wanted and what I wanted too.

After a few weeks of similarly indecisive dates, Neil finally asked me to go home with him after a midnight showing of *Fantasia*. Each of us had a relationship with a past lover that was unresolved at some level, and during the next month, after visiting our ex-boyfriends, without talking about it, we chose each other instead. We have been together ever since, celebrating our sixteenth anniversary in 1996.

Since I moved in with Neil after graduating from Georgetown, we have moved six times: once from Washington, D.C., to Massachusetts, and then five times within Massachusetts, in pursuit of new jobs and graduate degrees. Helping each other as much as possible emotionally and financially, we have weathered two master's programs and one doctoral program between us. Since we met, both of Neil's parents and one of his grandmothers have died, and my brother died. Supporting each other through these losses expanded and deepened the closeness we already felt as sexual and romantic partners.

Just before our fifth anniversary, Neil and I had a commitment ceremony in the hall of a Unitarian church. Almost all of our immediate family members attended (the two families meeting for the first time) as well as most of our dearest friends. We were surprised by how much this ceremony helped some of our relatives accept us as a couple. Neil's father, an All-American in football *and* basketball and a lieutenant colonel in the Air Force, made an impromptu speech, saying that in spite of his difficulty over the years accepting first Neil's homosexuality and then me, he was impressed by all the love in Neil's life both from Neil's friends and from me. He said that he had grown to welcome rather than resent me. Several of our guests were brought to tears by this unexpected and emotional tribute to the happiness that proud and open gay life and love can bring.

SURF'S UP

by Paul George Wibands

The day we met might more appropriately be thought of as the days we met: I remember one day as our first meeting, and he remembers another.

The first "first" was a sunny summer day. I was on the enormous one-block strip of Virginia Beach, Virginia, that in the early seventies was frequented by gay men. It was a fairly routine visit; I lived just a few blocks away and always shopped for a mate while sunning and swimming. I longed for the proverbial cottage with the white picket fence and a working man who lived and breathed just for me.

Making my way out into the midsize waves, I looked around with each little jump that helped avoid a mouthful of salt water. My technique for making acquaintances was woeful at best...but I tried. I always aimed for single individuals and avoided couples or groups — that usually narrowed the pack down considerably! There he was, a bit shorter than I am, causing his jumps to be a bit more energetic than mine. We exchanged small talk about the day and the water, and then I cut to the chase with, "Where are you from?"

"Baltimore," he replied.

Wrong answer, I immediately thought. *Not local, not relationship material.* Baltimore might as well have been the moon. I headed out of the water. He rejoined a group of guys that I hadn't realized he was with.

What I didn't immediately realize was that he was just as clumsy with the get-acquainted chat as I was and that though he was *originally* from Baltimore, he was now local — a fact I discovered on the second "first."

This was only a day or two later. I was again on the beach, this time for a late-afternoon swim. My timing was perfect — the crowds were gone, the sun wasn't excessively hot, and I had the day's work behind me. I spread my blanket just a few feet from the line left by the receding tide and looked out on the waves. There, bobbing about, was a lone male figure. I made my way out to within earshot just in case conversation might float between the two of us. We spoke a few words, and I soon recognized him as Mr. Baltimore. *Damn, the weekend's over,* I remember thinking. *What's he still doing in town?*

We frolicked a bit in the surf, and I soon realized that his white bathing suit was virtually transparent, a fact to which he seemed oblivious. Heading back to my blanket, I insisted he stop and accept a towel to cover himself. Alas, I had fallen victim to his lifelong fetish of scandalizing through exhibitionism.

He sat down and visited for a while. Ultimately we agreed to go back to my place, a feat not without a few bumps. My parents were visiting and staying at my apartment, so I called and convinced my sister to invite them over *immediately.* She was a bit dense at first but finally got my drift. As we pulled into the apartment complex, my parents were pulling away.

THE DAY WE MET

What followed next was some of the most miserable sex I've ever had: Both rank amateurs, we had no idea what titillated each other. To make matters worse, there was sand all over us and all over the bed. Somehow, it never occurred to us to shower first.

At the time, we convinced ourselves that it was great fun. I learned that he was recently discharged from the Navy and was indeed in town to stay. Friendship blossomed…then love bloomed…and twenty years later we are still blissfully together.

JAVA MEN
by Michael Dubson Sage

T im and I met in December 1983 in a Presbyterian
Church in Champaign, Illinois. We were both attending a gay and lesbian coffeehouse, a weekly event
sponsored by the Gay and Lesbian Illini, the student organization at the University of Illinois. I'd been out to myself
for several years, but I'd been living in Decatur — the perfect wall-to-wall closet for a young gay person who desired
a life. Because I wanted to be a member of a gay community, to find gay friends, and, most of all, to find a steady
boyfriend with whom I could build a life, I moved from
Decatur to Champaign in October 1983 because of the gay
bars there and the gay student organizations and activities
at the university that welcomed nonstudents.

The first person I met in Champaign was Mike, a math
major at the university. I found myself instantly attracted to
him. He had a goofy-cute smile, broad shoulders, gorgeous
blond hair, and a frequent, eccentric laugh. He was warm
and friendly and seemed interested in everything I had to

say. It was Mike who introduced me to Tim, whom he'd brought to the coffeehouse for the first time. Mike said he'd had to coax Tim into coming. I assumed that meant Tim wasn't interested. Based on how they were treating each other and on remarks they made about shared experiences, my boyfriend-seeking mind deduced that Mike and Tim were a couple.

Tim was a lot different from Mike; he was tall and slender with long curly brown hair and long fingernails on his little fingers. He was cute in a sexy, shaggy way, with a rich baritone voice and an air of cool confidence about him. His words were measured, his smile was wide and boyish, and his laugh, when it came, was deep and real. Judging from his looks, I asked him if he was a musician. He laughed at the idea, and asked me if it was because of his fingernails; it turned out he did play the guitar. I told him it was because of the way he looked — a cross between Doug Henning and Tony Orlando. His looks and the elusive, confident air Tim kept about himself led me to believe that he was probably pretty wild. Aware of my stronger attraction to Mike, I quickly wrote Tim off as not my type. As the evening wore on, however, most of my preconceptions were overturned.

The first surprise was finding out that Tim was a graduate student in physics at the university. Nothing about him looked "physics" to me. He'd come to Illinois in 1979 from his home in Pittsburgh after graduating from Carnegie Mellon University.

The second surprise was that he had been reluctant to come to the coffeehouse because he was just coming out himself; this was his first foray into an openly gay environment. What I had seen as cool self-confidence was actually a lot closer to shyness, and he certainly wasn't wild.

The third surprise was that he and Mike weren't a couple at all but rather just good friends from the chess club. Tim had buried himself in his grad school work for five years and had avoided dealing with his sexuality. Mike, who was openly gay, had urged Tim to start coming out. Nevertheless, Mike was unavailable. He had a boyfriend who was out of town. I inwardly sighed with disappointment but went on with the evening.

The banter at the gay coffeehouse was light and loud, often silly and sometimes vulgar, and I spent most of the evening talking with Tim, Mike, and a young black woman named Nina, who described herself as being "a gay man trapped inside a lesbian's body." The church provided the space, but the members provided refreshments. That evening, I'd brought some store-bought cookies, and Tim had brought a plateful of homemade mocha nut butter balls. Mike and I took immense pleasure in teasing Tim about his butter balls.

Tim laughed at my jokes, asked me about my work (I was in restaurant management at that time), and wanted to know whether I was planning on going to college. Tim talked about his work and his plans to complete his Ph.D. and become a professor. He told me that he had yet to come out to his family and that his father was a Presbyterian minister. I felt empathy for him over that, having been burned by the mean side of Christianity myself.

The coffeehouse ended at ten, and afterward Tim, Mike, Nina, and I went to a nearby restaurant. It was cold out, and already there was plenty of snow on the ground. It felt really romantic and cozy as we walked down the sidewalks of campus, talking and joking, wrapped tightly in our coats as the biting air surrounded us and the snow crunched beneath our feet.

The conversation in the restaurant was just as wild and silly as before, with Tim and Mike both laughing regularly at my jokes and all three of us howling over the outrageous observations of Nina. Afterward Tim took us all home in his car. I was in the back with Nina, and Tim and Mike were in the front. I lived the closest, so Tim dropped me off first. When he pulled up in front of my apartment building, as I got out, I put my hand first on Mike's shoulder, then on Tim's to express my pleasure in having met them both and to say that I'd look forward to seeing them again at next Friday's coffeehouse. The simple touch of my hand on their shoulders, through the fabric of winter jacket and shirt, was as arousing for me as being in a locker room full of showering studs.

I went to the coffeehouse every Friday for the rest of December and saw Tim and Mike each week. My interest waned in Mike, but we became good friends. My feelings toward Tim, however, began to grow. I realized that he was exactly the kind of person I had been waiting for. I found him warm and quietly caring and a lot more emotional even than me. His commitment to his work ultimately inspired me to go back to college. He appreciated my humor and told me later that he thought I was a lot more real than a lot of the people at the coffeehouse. He was serious, very sweet, and as uninterested in casual affairs as I was.

Tim went home for Christmas, and when he came back after the first of the year, I was really glad to see him. We met each other at the coffeehouse every Friday, and my feelings of affection and desire for him were growing stronger each week. I did not, however, know how he felt about me. He was always pleasant and appeared to enjoy my company, but did that mean he was interested in me? I wanted to ask him out, but I was terrified. What if he said no?

On a Friday in late January, I was at the coffeehouse, watching another guy talking and flirting with Tim. Though Tim didn't seem to be responding, it made me nervous. What if somebody else got to him first?

The next morning, I called him to ask him out. I almost lost my nerve, tempted to hang up before or just after he picked up. When he did answer, I asked him if he'd like to go to a movie that evening, and he said — glory hallelujah — yes!

We went to see *Silkwood,* and afterward we went to a restaurant, where we talked for hours about the coffeehouse crowd, nuclear radiation, the world's evils, our work, our goals, our dreams, and Cher. This was the first time we'd ever been alone together, and the rapport between us was instant and easy. I loved his warmth, his laughter, his voice, his wit, and his smile, and I was ready to make another date.

After I took him home, I asked him to dinner at my apartment later that week. He accepted. For the rest of the week, I relived the Saturday-night date and fantasized about the upcoming Thursday-night dinner, caught up in the romantic whirlwind of (maybe) finally having found a boyfriend.

The dinner was a big success. He got to meet my kitties, found out what a great cook I was, read some of my writing, and stomped the hell out of me in Scrabble. After the evening was over, I drove him home. Outside his apartment, in the car, I confessed that I really liked him and wanted to see more of him. Tim acknowledged that he had sensed that, that he did like me, but that he didn't want to rush into anything. We hugged, and I kissed him, and he kissed me, and it was wonderful.

The next evening, a Friday, I went to the coffeehouse, and there was Tim. I wanted to let it all hang out, but I didn't want to scare him off. After all, I'd been ready for this a lot longer than he had. After the evening was over, he invited me up to his place for tea and played his guitar for me. As I got ready to leave, wanting to be affectionate but nonthreatening, I went to kiss him good-bye. When I did, he put his arms around me, wouldn't let me go, and kept kissing me.

THE DAY WE MET

Whether or not he'd changed his mind, he was rushing; I didn't go home that night. Our relationship as a couple officially began in the early hours of that January morning in 1984. Over the next few months, it grew stronger and more solid, and we've been together ever since.

WE'LL ALWAYS HAVE PARIS

by David Watmough

Floyd and I, a Californian and an Englishman, respectively, live in Vancouver, Canada, and have done so for over thirty years. We met in Paris, on the twenty-fifth of September 1951, in the chaplain's study of St. George's Anglican Church.

To be honest, I have had to estimate the precise date, for all I recall with chronological certainty is that our second meeting was at High Mass in the French capital on the Feast of St. Michael and all the Angels that same year. And Michaelmas is celebrated on September 29.

It had to be a Wednesday because that was when Father had a social evening for any English-speaking students resident in Paris who were disposed to drink sherry and chat. I was living on the premises at the time. It was two years after my graduation from King's College, London University, and I had celebrated my twenty-fifth birthday the previous month in Cornwall, where I grew up.

I have further reason to remember what was to become

the most momentous day in my life in that I was suffering from a toothache — so much so that shortly after dinner, before the guests were scheduled to appear, I informed my fellow student living in the clergy house that I had decided not to appear at the soiree but would pop an aspirin and take to my bed instead. Indeed, I was in the process of doing this when Keith bounded up three flights of stairs and, with his usual ebullience, insisted that I stop undressing and return with him to the already assembling company in the book-lined study.

"My dear, you've *got* to come down. A whole bunch of Americans has arrived, and one is just right for you! As soon as I saw him, I just knew it. He is tall and blue-eyed, with a lovely smile. And he's from California. What more could you want! Of course, I'm not sure he's *die Forelle* (that was a code name Keith and I used meaning gay), but he's with an older guy who I swear is."

But my tooth really hurt. I wasn't about to be easily persuaded by the ever-enthusiastic Keith. On the other hand, nor was he about to yield to my self-pity. He picked up my slippers from where I'd kicked them off, found my pullover similarly discarded, and told me at least twice more how handsome the Californian student recently enrolled at the Sorbonne was.

"Well, OK," I mumbled grudgingly. "But I warn you, if these aspirin don't work, I'm coming back here to bed."

The funny thing is, I have no more recollections of that toothache. I don't even recall visiting the dentist over it. When I entered the now fairly crowded room, it was to confront some dozen or so students, both young men and women, milling about Father, who sat in his leather armchair, a brandy snifter in his hand as they paid him court.

It was a familiar enough scene, as both Keith and I had been living in the *presbytère* for the past two years and had attended scores of such functions. What separated the occasion from any other took place the moment my sight traversed the room to where Floyd was standing, dressed, I remember, in chinos and a wool plaid tartan shirt. For in those brief seconds of appraisal, I knew with hard certainty that after all my years of cruising — since I was thirteen or so — I was looking at the man I immediately wanted to be my partner for life. He was my opposite: tall, smilingly relaxed, and not self-conscious — all traits that have never departed him.

This was real life. Floyd was in Paris for further education, not looking for marriage or its gay equivalent. He was barely out and was not yet twenty-one. I quickly became the persistent suitor, and within a year I pursued him to California and then back to Europe when Uncle Sam claimed him as a French interpreter during the Korean War.

Our relationship did not really stabilize until he was working on a Ph.D. at Stanford and I was writing professionally in San Francisco. But even in those initial cruel separations, we wrote each other almost every day.

From the cover of my current novel, *The Time of the Kingfishers,* there beam two youths standing on the parapet of St. Germain-en-laye on the outskirts of Paris. That's us: Easter, 1952. Then and now. It's all good. Floyd agrees.

THE FRENCH HAVE A WORD FOR IT

by Anonymous

I'll never forget the first day I met "Whit." It felt like serendipity, because I was not looking for a man at all. I had taken a position in August as a staff member at a major university. A few days later, business required my presence in the offices of the university's law review, a student publication. Shortly after my arrival there, in walked a most distinguished-looking "youngish" man.

As it turned out, he had just arrived back on campus from a summer teaching position at a West Coast university. His rapport with the law review men (yes, it was *men* in those days of long ago) was remarkable; it was abundantly clear that they were delighted to see him. His pleasure in the reunion was equally manifest, his face flush with the most genuine of smiles I had ever seen.

We were introduced. My heart leaped in my chest from the moment of this encounter, for I had seen enough of his appearance and warm personality to feel instantly what the French call a *coup de foudre* (a thunderbolt — that is, love at first sight). It wasn't just his smile or his hearty laugh or his gentle eyes or his handsome face or his presence: I perceived him to be a truly charismatic figure.

After a brief conversation with Whit in the presence of a number of other men who probably did not share our orientation, I completed my transaction in the law review office. I left feeling I had never met anyone so immediately and so powerfully attractive, but I warned myself, *Get hold of yourself. You can't be so lucky as to meet Mr. Right in these surroundings; you are just infatuated. A day or two, and you'll see how imaginary your thunderbolt was.* But my heart wouldn't stop singing over what might come to be.

Whit was a man of easy confidence; he possessed a warm and engaging manner, which made him immediately attractive to virtually everyone he met. His smile and laughter were contagious. He had a way of putting everyone at ease but always hungry for further contact. I certainly felt that hunger as keenly as I have felt any hunger in my life.

In the days that followed, he clearly seized the initiative. He came to my office with startling frequency but always in the context of seeking my assistance. Yet I knew he wasn't helpless. I responded professionally but warmly and did my utmost to make these contacts appear routine to any casual observer. I knew that they were anything but routine, and I'm sure gave off clues to that effect. I inwardly sensed that he felt as attracted to me as I knew I felt toward him. And I am certain that he identified the day of our meeting in his memory as being just as significant to him as it was for me.

In retrospect, I realize that my efforts to conceal the repeated contacts as routine would never garner me nomination for an Academy Award. The situation must have been transparent to at least one female coworker who reported in something of a snit to a mutual acquaintance that I was "too good-looking." (She was interested in him too.) Just guess what that code phrase was meant to indicate in those days.

But these "professional" contacts were all there was — until he asked me out for dinner. The dinner was excellent, the conversation stimulating, and that first physical contact (a kiss) sensational. Our emotional and physical reactions toward each other had already moved us both far enough along that there did not seem to be any reason to delay complete physical exploration of each other. Whit literally swept me off my feet and carried me to his bed. After that first night I knew I would never again look for another man.

We began spending all our free time together, starting with weekends. Our friendship flowered quickly; by Christmas he was insisting on celebrating the twelve days of Christmas by giving me a mini gift every day. Within the year we were planning all our summer trips together. We agreed that it would be inadvisable to live together, since in our immediate environment such an arrangement would attract unwanted attention and invite speculation.

Whit was eight years older than I, and one of the great attractions he possessed was his vast grounding in art, music, and theater. He shared his insights with me without restraint. I learned so much from him in all those areas, and he helped immeasurably in informing my tastes. He could walk through a museum and see ten times as much as I took in. It was always such a pleasure to measure my own reactions to art, architecture, music, theater, and ballet against his, and I learned so very much in the process. He was truly a liberal education for me, and for this I shall never cease being grateful. Most of conscious life is, after all, lived away from bed. Whit was active on the boards of an opera company, a ballet, and an art museum.

This idyll went on for twenty-one years. Honestly, I never looked at another man during that whole period. Every year that passed yielded an increasing and a profound assurance in me that my life had been joined to that of the most magnificent of God's creatures. We had speedily absorbed the ability to know what the other was thinking and to complete each other's thoughts. We truly lived one life. We talked of our eventual retirement and where we would go to spend our retirement years.

However, during this time, Whit learned that he had a genetically induced terminal illness. Initially he chose not to be "out-front" with me about the seriousness of his illness, but eventually I shared his knowledge of his condition. That gave us a chance to savor the bittersweet winding down of his life.

He underwent indescribable suffering, bravely borne, and he ultimately died. It is then that I wished we had lived together.

At his death, I simply did not know how I could go on living. I felt my loss to be devastating. The matter was made infinitely more painful for me by the knowledge that Whit never wanted anyone to know of his consistent attraction to me. Thus, there was no one to whom I could open my heart, not even to the clergy of the parish to which we both belonged, to which I had introduced him, and in which he had become fully and significantly involved. Being in a closet is bad in ordinary circumstances, but it is truly torture when a person is undergoing grief on his own.

It took me approximately four years before I could even adjust to the concept of going out to see whether I might find another man. Having been joined in a union so total in its exclusivity to a man I could not hope to replace, I did not feel comfortable in going out to any of the usual gay haunts. Four years of extreme loneliness gradually ended when I perceived that Whit would not have wanted me to mourn endlessly for him.

THE DAY WE MET

Five years after Whit's death, I met a man who had great magnetism and charm, and we have now joined our lives for ten years. It can be no slight to him that I have centered my "first meeting" account on Whit. Life is not a record that plays over again exactly the same; and distance from the event makes it easier to relate my initial great love.

BEST-LAID PLANS
by Alex Michaels

"Brendan is on his way to your office," buzzed the voice over the intercom. My friend Brendan was coming to show me the guy that he had been "sort of dating." He had told me that he wanted me to meet this guy and to let Brendan know if I thought his friend is gay. I had to wonder how serious their relationship could be if Brendan didn't know the guy's orientation. To add to the tension, my father, who didn't know *I* was gay, was sitting in the office too.

When Brendan walked in, my initial reaction was to wonder where he found this beautiful man standing before me. He was blond, with gray eyes, dark skin, and a compact yet muscular body. He introduced himself as Jay. We talked for just a few minutes, but I knew I had to see him again.

After leaving, Jay asked Brendan if he wanted to invite me to go for drinks with them. They arrived as I was leaving work. We decided that we could relax more at my house.

Over the next few hours, Jay and I drank a little and talked a lot while Brendan, bored, went to sleep. I couldn't believe that Jay and I had so much in common. It was only halfheartedly that I reminded him that I was supposed to get up early the next morning. I was so surprised to hear him say, "Well, how about I just nudge you when it's time to get up?"

We spent the next six hours talking. Another friend, Daniel, dropped by, and he seemed to enjoy just watching us fall in love.

At dawn I stood in the kitchen talking to Jay and Daniel. We had all had a lot to drink by then. Jay suddenly stumbled backward, and when I caught him he went limp. I told him, "I won't let anything happen to you," and he put his lips to mine. It was the sweetest kiss I had ever known.

We kissed only briefly before we heard Brendan waking up. Jay went to talk to him, and I asked Daniel if what we were doing was wrong. A bit more jaded than I am, Daniel said, "Go for it, but don't expect to hear from him again." About that time, Brendan walked through and said he was exhausted, asking if I wouldn't mind taking Jay home. "Not at all," I answered quickly, even though I didn't plan to do so anytime soon.

I said good-bye to Brendan and Daniel and started toward my bedroom, where I heard the shower running. I walked the long hallway, excited yet afraid. The first sight of Jay in the shower — naked, wet, and holding his arms out to me — is permanently burned into my memory. I stripped quickly and stepped into those arms. I had never felt safer in my life. We spent over an hour in the shower, emptying the hot water heater twice.

Later we crawled exhausted from the shower and slipped, still wet, between the sheets. I was worried for a moment when Jay rolled from me, but he thrilled me when he reached back and pulled my arm over him. We lay there only a moment before he said, "Nothing in my life has ever felt so right." I knew exactly what he meant.

We made love several times over the next few hours, alternating passion and sleep. It was noon when we realized that I wasn't going to make it to work and that we were both really hungry. I ordered some food as Jay nibbled parts of my body, trying to distract me. We now had thirty more minutes of passion before a delivery man would be at my door. We took advantage of it until the doorbell rang.

With Jay's promise to feed me in bed ringing in my ears, I made the trek down that hallway that took me to him earlier. I was shocked to find my parents standing at the door. They were shocked to see me standing there in a towel. Mom explained that she was sorry for waking me but that they just *had* to show me the results of their latest shopping spree. Taking advantage of her version of the story, I told her that I had, in fact, just woken up. I jumped, however, when my dad began heading toward my room, muttering something about having to use my bathroom. Throwing myself in front of him, I asked if I could pull some clothes on first.

As I ran into my room, I knew I was ending this relationship as I apologized and asked Jay, "Could you please hide in the closet — just for a minute?"

He surprised me by laughing and saying, "But I just came out!" and stepping into my closet.

The ten minutes my parents were there seemed to last an hour. The situation was so absurd that I giggled the whole time. My parents thought their son had obviously been under too much pressure and had lost his mind. Their opinion didn't change when the delivery man showed up with "Lunch for two." I shrugged and smiled.

After they left I prepared myself for Jay's angry departure. When I retrieved him from my closet, though, all he said was, "Thank God. I'm starved!"

We sat in bed and ate our lunch, and at one point Jay turned to me and said, "With a great 'meeting story' like this one, we must have been meant to be together." More than two years later, I know that no one has ever said anything more true.

DELAYED AND DELIRIOUS
by Wayland Harper

I sipped the beer in front of me and changed expressions I thought appropriate to the monologue at my left. "Jeweler" and I were drinking through the delay and transfer to train because of an Eastern Airlines pilot strike. I hadn't gotten his name, a salesman from St. Louis who wore his trade on the little fingers of both hands. The coffee bar in the hotel was empty except for the two waitresses, seated and having a tête-à-tête at the end of the counter, and a gentleman who had just entered and took a seat two stools away from me. We exchanged nods.

His dark pinstripe suit was set off by a paisley-print tie and well-shined shoes. We began an easy banter. His corn-flower-blue eyes all but snapped as he spoke in a soft Southern accent. His cataloging of me was obvious. I heard only the first name, Howard, as he extended his hand and moved to sit next to me, an easy conversation beginning. Our eyes periodically locked. I felt electricity, warmth, and mutual physical interest. Jeweler, I could sense, felt left out.

Our train to New Orleans was to depart from a station nearby, and Howard offered to drive us. We stayed for another drink, shared some common interests, and exchanged addresses. Was I to find here what I'd hoped for in San Francisco as I completed this vacation?

As we got our luggage to the car, at some point the backs of our hands brushed, then clasped together briefly, our palms sweaty and anxious as he wrestled with the keys to the car door. I tried projecting a casual calmness as we sat three in the front seat of his 1956 Bel Aire, our legs pressed tightly together. I could hear my heart pounding. Was he possibly as excited as I was?

The long train ride was a restless one, with returning thoughts and pictures: his short-cropped hair, his boyish profile, his apple chin — even the music we'd spoken of, *Carmina Burana*, played in the spinning orbit of my mind. I would have to write him immediately upon my return, to let him know more about me and to gain answers to the questions jamming my mind. We knew nothing of each other but that we were attracted physically and intellectually. I was a bit frayed and travel-worn compared with his crisp appearance, but we shared similar tastes in our attire. His Nordic blondness made me feel dark by comparison.

I had few friends who would understand my excitement over this man. There was no one I could talk to about Howard. My first letter filled several pages of confessions and hopes both professionally and personally. I also suggested he visit me in my summer rental in Florida. The letter on its way, I looked for other things to think about. I turned to my sketchbook, lifted from it a pencil rendering, and worked it into a watercolor of the little house in which I lived, improving the actual appearance with imagined vines, shrubs and splashes of sunlight against dense tropical foliage.

Two weeks went by, and several of our letters passed en route. We were writing daily. I found myself cherishing each letter, stacking them away neatly in a drawer after I'd answered each one. Some questions were answered, some answers inferred. Our closings had become "Love." He took me up on my invitation but only for a long weekend. It would be short, but it would *be* — and in just five more days.

My newly inspired watercolor turned out quite nicely. I decided I'd have it mounted and present it as a gift to Howard, a memento of our first time together in my little twenty-five-dollar-a-month house. Though I had a rather prestigious address, private and well-secluded, my little house was set off a carriage-house drive and a bit humble.

It was a beautiful June night of the summer of 1960 that my MG Roadster hummed along on its way to the airport. What an evening to meet a lover…*lover, commitment, lifetime sharing* — word clusters that permeated my thinking. Words that I had not said aloud pushed their way to my attention. I took a deep breath and tried not to admit that I was a bit scared.

Was he taller than I, would I recognize him, could he be asking himself the same questions about me? We had been together so briefly. His mouth and well-polished teeth reminded me of that young senator, John Kennedy. I couldn't miss him.

I stood inside the gate at the foot of the ramp and saw him immediately as he flashed that smile. I waved and waited, then suddenly our hands touched in a firm handshake that warmed me like an embrace.

Dialogue came easily as we sat close in my small car and sped away from Tampa International Airport, remembering our first ride together. The canopy of night above us was generously punched-out in stars. I felt good in my Florida color with hair bleached by the sun.

Tropical smells brushed us as we arrived outside my door. A faint glow emanated from inside the bamboo-curtained windows. Entering through the small, galley-type kitchen, we stopped, took frosted glasses from the freezer, and shared a Champale.

"The night that I met you," I toasted. We drank and then, without another word, kissed deeply and held each other.

The following April, now back in Houston, we were confirmed into the Episcopal Church with a ritual neither of us had anticipated. After kneeling together before a priest and being blessed, we knew this was the closest thing to a marriage ceremony we could expect for two men in 1961.

As I look back on this courtship and good fortune, a special meaning comes to this relationship, rather carelessly begun, always remembered from that fateful summer.

THE WAY WE ARE

by Richard Allen May

A t first glance, my soon-to-be lover absolutely terrified me. He suddenly stepped out of the shadows beneath a stairway to Tower Records and glared at me. I'm sure my eyes must have bugged out; I know my mouth popped open. The look on his face was so stern. He was exceptionally blond, decked out in an olive drab shirt, camouflage pants, and kick-ass boots. I almost ran.

We had spoken once, over the phone, to arrange this meeting or date or whatever it was. I had answered his personal ad. ROBERT REDFORD I'M NOT... it began. He sounded so sweet over the phone. He said he was an artist. I was expecting Leonardo, not Rambo. Before I headed for the hills, however, he managed to speak and smile, and we began a rambling conversation that has lasted seven years now.

What attracted me to Robert at first was his sense of humor. His ad was funny. However after I had recovered from the initial shock of seeing him, I noticed how well-built he was — and he still is, after years of erratically fanatical gym duty. He also has the most beautiful blue eyes, softened by gray.

Still, even though he's built and I'm a Scorpio, sex has never been a major part of our relationship. Maybe it's because we were in our early forties when we met, apparent survivors of an AIDS-scourged generation. Sex had become serious, even dangerous. Besides, we had done the hormonal thing and both believed sex too often confused the issue of getting to know each other. But after agreeing that we "no longer had sex on the first date," we promptly went to Robert's place and had sex. And then we cuddled. I was impressed: Robert is a champion cuddler-snuggler. He's very physical — touching, holding, wanting to be connected. The warmth and substance of him always amazes me because his demeanor is often so tough. It's a defense mechanism.

It wasn't love at first sight. I've experienced that, and it was wonderful but didn't last. The love that Robert and I share had a rocky start and has frequently been threatened by our independent natures and the heavy baggage we both carried. Several times we almost spun apart. Robert swears he once broke up with me; if so, I must not have been paying attention.

Communication has been our big lesson. He has learned to communicate verbally with me even when he doesn't want to. (Sometimes I wish he weren't such a good student.) And I've learned to be more conscious and corrective of how I communicate: the tone of my voice, my choice of words. He has anger problems. I have budgetary difficulties. All God's children have some kind of problems. Solving them is part of the fun.

Robert would not remember this first meeting exactly as I have. I am sure that I was not dressed in any way to cause sudden alarm. He remembers how attractive I looked. Ha! I have a big nose, unruly hair, and a set of teeth that makes dentists see dollar signs. But love works miracles; it has with us. Neither one of us is Robert Redford, and neither one of us cares.

LOVE CONNECTION

by Brian Treglown

"Hey, Brian, I'm having a brunch this Sunday. I want you to come. Are you free?" The call was a welcome one. Tim was a good friend, and the brunch would be fun. More important, I was down in the dumps and needed a pick-me-up. I'd recently had a six-year relationship go bad — that's a nice way of saying I'd gotten dumped — and getting out of the house was just what I needed.

As Tim described what he had in mind, I got more and more enthusiastic. "Besides you, I'm inviting three other guys," he said. "They're all single, eligible, and looking. At the very least you should get a date out of it."

Visions of *The Dating Game* ran through my head. In my mind I was sitting with Jim Lange, who was asking me stuff like: "Bachelor Number One, if we're having dinner in a candlelit restaurant and I reach over and grab your hand, what would you do?" or "Bachelor Number Three, would you object to my Great Dane sleeping on the bed with us?"

By Sunday my anticipation was heightened. I was having a good hair day, and I felt suave, witty, and thin — ready to make my *Dating Game* selection.

Tim greeted me at the door with the news that Bachelor Number One had canceled. A minor disappointment but not a big deal. (I have since met Bachelor Number One. He is cute, intelligent, and has a horrible drinking problem. Somebody must have been looking out for me). But, Tim added, the other two were there. "Hang up your jacket and come join us."

So the four of us sat in the living room, taking in Tim's spectacular view overlooking Lake Michigan. Bachelor Number Two was indeed cute. He ran a training program for a large corporation that he started talking about. And he talked. And he talked. It was kind of interesting, but plain and simple it was more information about training programs than I needed to know. Yes, Bachelor Number Two was certainly successful in his career, but he was also an egomaniac who seemed to really like the sound of his own voice. It was during this monologue that he called conversation that I snuck my first peek at Bachelor Number Three.

Hmm...cute...professional-looking...sandy-colored hair...wire-rimmed glasses...a short, trim mustache. The more Bachelor Number Two talked about himself, the more I began to wonder about Bachelor Number Three.

His name was Carl, and he was "into computers," I learned. He was from Ohio and had come to Chicago to go to graduate school. As so often happens, he had come out and decided this was a good place to stay. He'd dated a bit but hadn't had a relationship. He was a real sweetheart with a friendly, warm smile and a down-to-earth outlook on life. He liked movies, Stephen Sondheim, and hairy chests. And no, he wouldn't mind if my Great Dane slept with us on the bed. This was getting better all the time.

And the great thing was that he seemed as interested in me as I was in him. When our eyes locked for the first time, there it was — electricity. When he talked it was totally unself-conscious. No careful choosing of words or plotting out what people's reactions would be. The more he talked, the more attracted I got. The mustache, legs, and spectacular tush didn't hurt either.

I was sensing that this could be it. *That's crazy,* I told myself. *You haven't even gone out with him.* But, hey, I sure was forgetting about everything and everyone else in the room. Remember Carly Simon's song "Anticipation"? That's how I felt. As Tim served up the mushroom quiche, I made my decision. I would ask Bachelor Number Three out. As we were leaving the brunch, I asked for and received Carl's phone number.

Our date was set for the following Saturday. Carl had invited a group of friends to Rodgers and Hammerstein Night at Ravinia, Chicago's outdoor theatre. The evening was a fiasco.

First of all, everyone had been given a location at which to meet. But Rodgers and Hammerstein are a big draw; the place was mobbed. We never found any of the others until well into the concert. Second, it was hot; muggy, humid, and beastly hot. Shirts were drenched, hair was matted with sweat, and everybody was uncomfortable as hell. The heat turned the cheesecake I'd made to impress Carl into something the consistency of tomato soup. Tomato soup that ran all over my pants and the trunk of Carl's car, I might add. Virtually nothing went right.

Yet in the midst of all these traumas, Carl was cool. He just shrugged off the problems with his winning smile, and by the end of the evening, I was hooked.

On the way home Carl said he would like to meet my Great Dane. I had to admit that I didn't have one; that I slept alone. Would he like to join me?

This summer we'll celebrate our twelfth anniversary. We're still as much in love as ever. But instead of a Great Dane, it's our cat, Audrey, who sleeps with us.

A CAN OF PEAS, A BAG OF RICE — AND THOU
by Craig M. Machado

I met my partner of fourteen years, Dick, at a church —
an unlikely venue, some would contend, given the
incessant volley of antigay hysteria hurled from those
hallowed (hollowed) halls of Christendom. But as I discovered, there are many strands of Christians, and the ones
I hooked up with were committed social activists — peace
and justice mongers par excellence. They were also unflag-
ging in their affirmation of gays and lesbians. As it turned
out, both Dick and I were looking for a community of people held together with more than the trendy platitudes of
the greedy 1980s.

I moved to San Francisco in the late '70s from Menlo Park,
California, after a string of post-Peace Corps jobs and loves.
I spent two torturous, unfulfilling years with one of them,
Paul. We had some good times, but I was terribly naive, easily taken advantage of, and constant prey to my own insecu-
rities, which kept me clinging to someone not interested in
a long-term, mostly monogamous relationship. San

Francisco, aside from its "gay mecca" allure, offered me the hope of finding a bona fide soul mate.

But the candy-store syndrome of gay San Francisco began to wear me down after a while. I needed more in my life than bars and baths and cute men with too much attitude. I wanted to meet someone unpretentious, someone real: a lover of books, ideas, conversation, political engagement, walks, travel, cooking. These requisite components of "that special one" were not, at the time, perfectly coalesced into the composite man of my dreams. Rather, I carried fleeting ideas, urges, and images of many "someones" as I wandered through the cool, mist-strewn streets of the city.

One night I wandered into the Network Coffee House, a funky '60s basement of an apartment building that served as a refuge for some of the weird, wired, homeless, derelict, spiritually searching, nonconformist folk that lived in San Francisco. Through the Coffee House I met Scott and Glenda, codirectors of San Francisco Network Ministries. Glenda was also serving as part-time pastor for a shrinking congregation of Presbyterians in the Sunset/Golden Gate Park area and asked me to try out the church.

One Sunday at coffee hour, shortly after I had started going to church, Scott introduced me to Dick. Nervous and shy, he shook my hand. He was a reporter for one of the city's gay papers, the *Sentinel.* Coffee cups in hand, we chatted, and slowly common interests began to move our conversation beyond the mundane. It was not love at first sight but a gradual, mutual warming to each other.

I ran into Dick again a week or so later on the street. He was out campaigning for a local politician. He reminds me of that meeting often when we're telling someone how we met. "You didn't seem to care a hoot about me," Dick will say, half joking, half serious. While I can conjure up the encounter, I can't put an exact finger on how I felt. Aloof?

THE DAY WE MET

Absorbed by some trivia of the day? Or was it that Dick was pursuing me and I didn't get it?

We met again several weeks later at a church-sponsored retreat. The exact theme of the retreat escapes me, but it was to be a day of quiet self-reflection punctuated by readings, discussion, and lunch. Talking between periods of silence, we were, by the end of the day, comfortably at ease with each other. I don't think either of us had a clear idea of where things might go, but we both agreed we were hungry and decided to eat dinner together.

We ended up at Dick's studio because I had nothing to eat at my place and because between us we had about five dollars. Dick found that his "gourmet cache" was depleted, but he threw together a meal both of us still laugh over — rice, canned peas, tuna, and a bottle of beer we shared. We sat around a coffee table in the cozy glow of candlelight on tie-dyed pillows, knees beginning to rub, faint flickers of lust rising between bites. After that, our bowls set aside, coffee table pushed back, we stretched out on his futon, and our hands began to wander under shirts and down pant legs. Then came tentative kisses and fumbling with zippers... We awoke the next morning, predictably not refreshed but quickly revived with coffee, to the insistent chatter of Dick's finches.

And so began six months of courting until the day we set up house together (the date we also acknowledge as our unofficial "marriage") in a railroad flat in the Mission district with a skyline view of downtown from the back porch. Now we live in Oregon, which for the past five years has provided many challenges (in particular, two antigay ballot measures).

It may not have been love at first sight, but love it has steadfastly grown into — and love it gently endures.

ANNIVERSARILY CHALLENGED

by Michael Austin Shell

I am something of a curmudgeon. I certainly don't like to let on how important romance is to me. Even so, my first three long-term affairs were all of the love-at-first-sight variety. Life and love with each of these men was rich and unique, with many shared blessings. It's also true, however, that from my side at least, the relationships were too fantasy-based. I didn't know how to sustain them as the fantasy parts shifted and faded.

Jim and I have been committed to each other for more than ten years. We've known each other much longer. When friends ask how we first got together, we usually joke that it depends on when we start counting. We first met in 1965 as high school sophomores. I hadn't understood yet that I was gay, and anyway, Jimmy wasn't the teenage jock type I longed to do God-knew-what with. He was a good friend, though, and I did find him sweet and intelligent. He was more self-aware than I but still closeted — this was, after all, pre-Stonewall Bible Belt country. He tells me I was dorky and cute. He likes boys with glasses.

Fast-forward to 1978. After ten years up north, I'd returned home and was moving into a duplex with my second lover, a boyish, 30-something animal lover named Stephen. There, next door, was this skinny bearded fellow with a gentle nature and a goofy, teasing sense of humor. It was Jim, living with his lover, Randy, whom he'd met at the Metropolitan Community Church. Still no sparks flashed between us, but we were becoming fast friends once again.

Spring 1980. I'd worked a year overseas in Saudi Arabia and was traveling with Nikki, whom I'd met in England. We stopped briefly to see my old neighbors. This was when Jim and I stumbled into our first burst of passion for each other.

One night while the other two chatted, he and I fell into a kiss. The experience was sudden and heated. Before it had ended we were making love on the sofa. Then we broke off, ashamed that we'd not honored our partners by asking them first. It took us all a while to talk this out. Both couples survived, and we parted as friends.

Back from travels a year and a half later, I crashed temporarily with Randy and Jim. "Temporarily" turned into four years in a house we called the Seminary, both because of our spiritual interests and because we were now three single men growing into a family. During those years — coinciding with grad school for me — we three learned to sustain a deep companionship and nonsexual love. Sometimes we chuckled at the puzzlement of our friends, who wondered who was sleeping with whom.

In fact, though, this was also the period when Jim says he fell in love with me. I, in turn, was drawn, both to the personal warmth of this man and to his radiant physical warmth the few times that we did make love. He began to court me, but I kept saying no. I was focused on school and career, and he still wasn't my type.

Nineteen eighty-five. My first year on a counseling job in another city. I was feeling whole and self-confident, more open than ever. When Jim finally came for a visit, we spent a long evening in the home of a mutual friend. I lounged on the floor at his feet while a group of us watched some movie on TV. I don't know what triggered the shift in me. Everything I knew about him came together so clearly. There was a simple truth: What I really wanted in a partner was already available. I leaned back against his legs. He lay a hand on my shoulder. We knew without saying what had happened.

The years since have brought many occasions for meeting each other afresh. I don't hold him to old fantasy expectations, so he keeps surprising me with lovable quirks I would never have looked for. For example, he readily points out for me boys he knows are my type — and I reciprocate. I think you can see why I ask, "When do we start counting?"

SEEING RED

by Jeffrey M. Hannan

I have a decades-long history of hating Halloween. As a child I despised trudging through our hilly neighborhood in a sweaty mask and flammable costume to have a fistful of gratuitous kindness dumped in my plastic pumpkin. As a teenager I loathed slathering shoe polish on my little brother's face and telling him he looked cool so I could trudge him around the neighborhood for another ten years of the same supercilious ingratitude. In my twenties, free of the suburban requirement, I moved to San Francisco and managed to avoid October thirty-first — either by volunteering to work the night shift or by staying in to watch a movie in the dark — with curmudgeonly success.

At thirty, however, my antipathy for the hallowed season abated, albeit ever so slightly. It was All Castro's Eve, the Saturday before Halloween and perhaps the holiest of holy days in the Castro. All Castro's Eve is the raucous opening night of the long celebration of masks and feathers, sequins and leather, fishnets and baby-smooth bottoms. It is the residents' party, a night of celebration for locals only, before the streets are blocked off on Halloween night proper, choked with busloads and carloads of suburban gawkers, Japanese tourists, and troublemakers.

I was standing on the southwest corner of Eighteenth and Castro, one of the Western world's little Bethlehems, with my friend Ed, a Washington, D.C., native who was in town on business, and a colleague of his who was dressed up like a cleaning woman. Across the street a fabulously tall, lissome black drag queen in a hip-hugging marigold-yellow evening dress mimed pushing a Muni bus around the corner in front of Walgreen's. She dug her spike heels into the pavement and shoved effortlessly, to the cheers of the gathering crowd. I stood there, still slightly full of my pious contempt for masks (I'd never enjoyed dressing up and was glad others felt compelled to do it, thus alleviating me of my responsibility), but after having earlier viewed the spectacle of drag queens arriving in limousines and making grand, spotlit entrances into the Muscle Sisters Ball at the Collingwood Street School, my malaise had begun giving in to the celebration.

He appeared in red — a red down jacket — and we shook hands over a newspaper stand there on the corner. He was a friend of Ed's business associate, and it took me a couple of times hearing it to catch his name: Joaquin. Puerto Rican, I was told, now living in Berkeley. But he could just as easily have been a Plutonian residing in Birkenstocks. Fourteen years and half that many relationships had done me in. I may not have dressed the part, but I was a serious drag queen dragging around a trunkload of cynical torch songs. Joaquin was cute, but I decided I could find cute in a five-dollar magazine if I wanted it. I could do without any relationships.

But something happened later on in a bar called the Phoenix. The three of us — John (the business associate), Joaquin, and I — went for a drink after about an hour of milling about on Castro. (We'd left Ed, entranced, out on the street to continue his immersion in the spectacle.) We had a drink and chatted, although I mostly just listened and wondered whether my water had no scotch in it or my taste buds were as dead as my libido. Then, in reference to his political activities of late, Joaquin said half jokingly, "I'm climbing the Berkeley political ladder." I felt a sudden shudder in my body as though all of my buttons had been simultaneously pushed. I looked over at him and discovered a genuinely adorable face and sexy, stocky body emerging from the once-nebulous field of his red jacket.

Like Ed, I too am a native of Washington, D.C., and politics have always played a perverse, private role in my core of erotic associations. Suddenly, here was a man my own age with an engaging, sweet smile; beautiful brown eyes; a slightly self-mocking sense of humor; and a big red jacket with political ambitions posted all over it. And just when I thought all the good ones were married and living in Marin.

We opted to dance. Or rather, John and Joaquin did. I said I was going to order a real scotch and water first, then I'd join them out on the tiny, cramped floor. I downed my drink, went to the bathroom, and then stood overlooking the dance floor as if biding my time for some unknown, yet imminently eminent, purpose.

We no doubt made an odd trio dancing: John in his heels and feather-duster boa, Joaquin in his big red jacket, and I in my newfound, troubling nakedness. I'd had introductions before that left me in various states of dubious composure — with my pants around my ankles in a guest room at a housewarming party, for one — but I'd never been introduced to a man and so summarily dismissed him only to be reeled in a short while later by six seemingly innocuous words. Which is why when Joaquin's hand began grazing against mine on the dance floor, I felt it was my duty to let the touch linger. And occasionally take hold.

All throughout the dancing, I was speculating – and halfway hoping – that the night might be worthy of a journal entry the next morning. As usual, the old familiar voices of doubt and cynicism were running rampant in my head: *Maybe the touches are accidental; or worse, maybe he's genuinely interested.* In addition, there was a voice I'd never heard before, a voice that appeared repeatedly throughout my private writing but had never materialized inside my head. It said, *If you want something, go for it,* which was a sentiment I'd successfully brutalized myself with but rarely ever acted on – a dangerous drag I both wore and yet could not wear.

So on our way out the door to gather Ed from the streets, I asked Joaquin out for dinner the next week. He accepted.

By this time, Castro Street was smarting with drag queens and devils, witches and fairies, and muscle bunnies galore. As we wormed our way through the chaos and din, I realized that my malaise was lifting. It seemed the celebratory night was just that: a celebration, ambiguous and elusive.

On October twenty-second, All Castro's Eve, I began to discover that my history of hating Halloween was a history of personal denial. I'd worn hundreds of costumes throughout my life, none of which resembled me but all of which were crafted from the same perilous fabric I'd been gathering since my days as a dissatisfied child, lugging a plastic pumpkin around the neighborhood in search of genuine desire.

These days, though, my pumpkin, so to speak, is full. Full of good things: honesty, love, respect, and plenty of humor. Halloween is still my least favorite holiday, even though one year I won the prize for best noncostume. His name is

Joaquin, and he gives a whole new meaning to the expression "seeing red."

PARTY MEMBERS

Anonymous

In polite company we tell people we met at a party. While this is technically true, this statement omits the detail that it was a sex party: the regular Wednesday-night session of a safe-sex club, Premier Jacks.

I had been attending fairly regularly since being admitted to the group. Membership in this "private club" was not expensive, but you had to pass muster with the group's organizer, Jeff. All men who became members were required to meet at least one, if not all three, of the following criteria: You had to be attractive, well-built, and well-endowed. Jeff, being all three, was apparently well-suited to make these evaluations.

When I arrived that summer evening, I joined the others in checking my clothes (socks and sneakers excepted). I recognized some of the men from previous visits, but there were always new faces (and bodies) to notice and pursue. One man immediately caught my attention. I had never seen him at Premier Jacks before, but he met *my* three criteria: handsome, hirsute, and mustached. I watched him interact with others in the play area downstairs for a while and noticed he was not engaging in much sex play but was more of an observer. I took this to mean that he was either new to this type of event, shy, or both. Accordingly, I approached him cautiously rather than making any bold and potentially offensive moves.

I sidled up to him and joined him in watching a small cadre of other men enjoy some group play, and, seeing him take notice of me with apparent interest, gently began to massage his shoulders. I guess he was prepared for me to make the next move since he seemed at ease and responded by leaning back into me. He commented that I had wonderful hands, and I jokingly told him that I was a masseur. He found this fascinating, thinking I was one of those men who advertised as such in the back of our local gay paper, erotic photos included. (He later was quite disappointed to find out that I'm really an attorney — how dull.) This sparked a brief but lively discussion about erotic massages and sex clubs that led, inevitably, to our first sexual encounter.

I liked him instantly once we began talking. He has an easy, unpretentious way about him. His warmth and openness became more obvious to me when we continued our conversation on a comfortable couch upstairs (postsex, but still nude). We talked for a long time before deciding it was time to call it a night. After dressing, we traded business cards, which was when he found out I was not a masseur.

To this day, nearly eleven years later, when asked how we met, he continues to tease me about how I deceived him about my chosen profession at the "party." Not wanting to provide all the details of that night to whomever may be hearing his good-natured jibes, I usually laugh along and just say that I thought being a masseur was more exotic than being just another attorney. Plus, I figure it can be my fall-back occupation if ever I tire of lawyering.

FATE DATE

by Ken Lovering

I don't normally go for psychic, celestial, in-the-stars stuff. Knowing this, my friend Abby bought me an hour with a psychic one August before Paul and I met. She knew I would go because I can't resist such freebies. Surrounded by crystals and tea leaves, the great disseminator of hope told me that I would meet Brian, my soul mate, in Central Square, Cambridge, on October twenty-third. I didn't tell her two things that would make her prediction impossible: I was about to go to Europe for three months (I figured she was supposed to know that stuff); nor did I tell her my real name (she kept calling me Kevin, so I figured she had the wrong guy). My love of delicious irony stopped me from correcting her on both points.

My parents met on a blind date in a Howard Johnson's restaurant over thirty-five years ago. It's a simple story, really. They met, and they fell in love. Ditto with my brother and his wife. So when my friend Lisa called me over a year after my visit to the psychic ("Have I got a man for you!" she said when I picked up the phone), I felt — beneath my caution and pessimism — a compelling curiosity.

I was on the brink of resigning myself to lifelong solitude. Yes, I wanted to meet someone with whom I could spend my life, but I hated the work of dating: the making of plans, the anxiety, the primping, the anxiety, the getting to and from, the anxiety. What would I wear, say, and do? Would I like him? Would he like me? And would my worrying about all this preoccupy me to the point of social paralysis? Meeting someone else didn't seem worth all this even as I took Paul's phone number from Lisa. He had my number too, she said, so the rest was up to us. I, resistant to the whole idea, would wait for him to call me.

He didn't. And I couldn't get out of my mind that I was ignoring something important. But I didn't let anyone on to this. I didn't want to appear hopeful because I had just come out of two horrible dating experiences. One with another writer whom I had developed an embarrassing crush on, and another with a man who had developed an embarrassing crush on me. Crushes were too loud for me, the desperation that accompanies their possessive desire too violent. A crush suffocates, as the word itself implies, until there's nothing left but a rubbled heap of disillusion.

I met Paul by phone on a December Sunday. After pacing my apartment, I called him, nagged by the chance, however small, that he might be my soul mate. His voice was soft, a high baritone. We guardedly talked about books we liked and about our work (he was a health inspector, I a book-seller and writer in the midst of my master's thesis) and about how each of us would spend that Christmas.

He surprised me when he asked what I was wearing; I wasn't sure what he had in mind. On that lazy day I had on an old pair of jeans that had developed a large, stringy tear in the crotch. This intrigued him. He had on Sunday sweats and, to my relief, that was as far as that conversation went. I had caught him in the middle of laundry. Later, his landlord, a gay man who lived next door, was going to read his tarot. Did I believe in "that stuff"? I told him no. I thought it was just one more attempt to gain a false sense of control over the future, false because we can never really know where our lives will take us. We set up a time for dinner. He would pick me up at my apartment.

My then-roommate and longtime friend, Bonnie, does believe in "that stuff," and today it is an essential ingredient in the growing friendship between her and Paul. I've known him to phone her in Seattle (where she has since moved with her soul mate) after he has had a particularly intense dream. I value their connection, the fact that they get on so easily and without my prompting.

Around the time Paul and I first met, Bonnie's impending move to Seattle was a pressing issue in my life. Simply put, I didn't want her to go. But go she would, the following summer. I was sure I'd be lost after she left. Whom would I share myself with? Where would I live? She was — and remains — one of the very few people whom I trust completely.

On the night Paul was to arrive to pick me up for dinner, she was cooking in her matriarchal fashion and teasing me about my date while I primped myself and wavered between nonchalance and skepticism.

When the doorbell finally rang, Bonnie said in a singsong voice, "There's your da-a-ate!" and I responded in mock annoyance, "Yeah, yeah, yeah," as if this were the least important thing in the world to me. But an odd thing happened when I opened the door. Paul stood there in his blue winter jacket, his trimmed red beard the color of fire, his eyes bespectacled with serious gold frames. He was shorter than I and cute in a way that was both unique and familiar.

Though I knew I'd never seen him before, he felt startlingly familiar. I knew we didn't share a history, but I knew I could be comfortable and real with him. This frightened me to the point of dumbfoundedness. I tried to conceal my fear with small talk and greetings but when I brought him into the kitchen to meet Bonnie, the net that had been holding back my nervousness split wide open.

"This is Bonnie," I told him, "and, Bonnie, this is…" I motioned to him, figuring his name would progress naturally from my mouth, but my mind came up with nothing. We three stood there in a horrible, torturous silence while I squirmed and searched for his name in my memory. Who was he? Not even a bluff or some generic title (like "my date") came to mind. It was as if my panic had stripped me of language.

He must be insulted, I thought. *He must think he's just one more insignificant name on my crowded dance card.* I wanted to tell him that no one had ever done this to me before, no one had ever struck me stupid. But, of course, I couldn't speak. Bonnie saved me ("Paul, right?" she said), and I apologized later over appetizers so that my foible wouldn't hang over us all evening.

But the whole thing makes me think: Though I could never have realized it at the time, I was ripe to meet someone permanent. My resignation to a life alone meant that I was no longer out to impress. I wore no veneer or pretension that evening, so Paul knew exactly who faced him, and I got a pretty clear view of him too.

The timing, however, still puzzles me. Just as Bonnie was moving out of my life (geographically speaking), Paul was moving in. It seemed too perfect that I should have had someone to go to after she moved. What can be made of such things? It doesn't seem enough to merely be grateful; I want to know the workings behind it all. I want to know if

THE DAY WE MET

I'm being looked upon from some higher place to which only the most refined psychics have access. But if it's all random, dumb luck, I want to know that too.

NEVER SAY NEVER
by Grant Michael Menzies

I had resisted joining the gym for years, much as I had resisted learning anything about the arcane lore of computers — to me, direct contact with a metallic machine, stamping one's soul indelibly on crisp white bond, was the only way for a true writer to practice his art.

It goes without saying that as soon as I used a computer, the typewriter was banished to the closet to be brought out only on select occasions and then sent back to medieval darkness, where it belonged. And as time wore on, I came to see that even the gym might have a place in my life. I was a year past thirty, when your waistline ceases to correspond to your waistband, and I had to admit that vanity, which I had deplored in my faddish friends, indeed also had a place — wherever it would do the most good.

So, with these honorable intentions, I signed up at a local gym and then found that I couldn't go. This was distressing. We all know the feeling of paying for something and then not using it, what my Scottish grandfather would have termed "foolish waste" (as if there were a wise kind). But Grandfather had a point. I was paying; I should be using. My butt should be planted on those machines my dues were helping to maintain, and I should be doing laps in that pool that was, in some way anyway, mine by right. At last I called an old friend who knew me from my anti-gym days and asked his advice.

"Go to the gym!" he said after hearing my monologue.

"Oh, I will," I snarled. "I'm paying for it."

"You need some incentive," he replied calmly. "Just think — you might meet somebody nice there."

I laughed bitterly. So did he, but for a different reason. He had seen me through as many failed relationships as I had teeth (not counting the wisdom ones, perhaps mistakenly removed some years before). My habit of trying to meet Prince Charming at parties, at concerts, and through advertisements had yielded me naught but some good sex and an empty apartment to come home to each night. Why not try the gym?

I persisted in my hardheartedness. "Oh, sure," I said, "I'll meet someone the first night who'll go to the opera with me. Never."

"Never is a strong word," said my friend with that wise tone I had come to know and fear.

Well, I did say it. But I went to the gym that very evening. I had had a hard day at work, I was cranky, and I needed an endorphin rush. Before I knew it, I was walking through the locker room, fingering my key and eyeing some of the naked and dripping specimens standing on either side of me. *Nice dick,* I thought once, twice, ten times. *Dumb expression,* I thought five, ten, fifteen times. Was I being too hard on my fellow man? Wasn't sex really all one wanted or needed? Did it matter whether the boy of one's dreams, that husband to last a lifetime, knew who

Wagner or Verdi were or the difference between Bach and Rimsky-Korsakov?

When I first put the key into the lock, I figured I'd twisted it the wrong way — too much glancing aside at the bathing beauties slipping out of their Speedos. But no, I tried it again and again and began forcing it against its will. Nothing would open the locker. I knew the whole thing was a mistake. I stood there bundled up, bag on my shoulder, face red, while those laughing satyrs came and went about me, as if I were the museum gazer on display and they the works of art passing through.

I started toward the door (somebody at the desk would surely help me, or maybe I would leave and never come back) when somebody from behind said, "Need some help?" I focused on bright green eyes, black lashes, soft red lips, and a dark beard, trimmed. "Let me have your key," he said. Hairy arms, hairy hands. I watched him slip the key in. The locker opened. He turned to me. Pretty smile. "You just have to turn it the right way," he said. "I had the same problem."

"I was a little panicked," I tried to explain, as if that were the cause of my red face.

"It happens," he said.

"This is my first time here," I went on. Undressing was odd when the man standing before you was doing so for you with his eyes. "It was high time I came, though," I babbled on. *"Die Frist is um!"* I sang the first line of Vanderdecken, the haunted seaman in Wagner's *The Flying Dutchman*. "The time is up!"

"Und abermals verstrichen sind sieben Jahr," he sang.

I paused in amazement. "You know the opera?" I asked. "It's playing here in a few weeks. I can't wait to go."

"I *should* know it," he smiled. "I play piano for the opera company. Want to come to the dress rehearsal next week?"

THE DAY WE MET

I went to the rehearsal, and three months later Mark and I exchanged rings. When I called my parents that night, they were elated. I also called on my wise friend from yore. "What did I tell you?" said he. "Never say never!"

FRATERNALLY YOURS

by Steve Lane

"**C**an I give you a hand?" I looked up from the pile of leaves I had been raking. Deep blue eyes.

"Sure, but I think this is the only rake."

"My name is Mark Harrisson," he said, reaching out his hand. Warm, strong. I shook it.

"Steve Lane," I replied

"So," said Mark rhetorically. His youthful enthusiasm and disarming smile touched my subconscious in an uncomfortable place. I sublimated what I couldn't understand.

"There's some burlap in the garage," I quickly added. "We can load 'em up, but I'm not sure where to haul 'em.

"Maybe we can just dump 'em on Sigma Chi's lawn," Mark replied, laughing. Infectious. I knew then that I had found my best friend and partner in collegiate crime.

"Get to work, assholes!" growled a fraternity brother from a second-story window. We were pledges and targets for verbal abuse from the power-drunk members of the brotherhood.

"Sir, yes, sir!" we shouted, whipping into a chins-up, chests-out mock-military attention.

He continued his assault from the window.

"What are you?

"Cocksuckers, sir!" we replied in unison.

"And how long will you be cocksuckers?"

"A year!"

"A year what?"

"A year, *sir!*" we barked in unison.

The game was growing old.

"Now, get your butts out of my sight!"

"You been watchin' our butts, sir?" Mark said, grinning while he sensuously caressed his posterior. I glared at him. My arms already ached from the push-ups I'd been put through for insubordination.

"I'll bust your butt, Harrisson! Now, get out of my line of vision!"

"Sir, yes, sir!"

We left our feigned subservience dangling as we beat a hasty retreat. Pushing and shoving our way to the garage, we noticed the pledges from the neighboring Sigma Chi house performing the same Friday-afternoon cleanup ritual before the night's party. They were probably conspiring to dump *their* leaves on *our* lawn. Half-heartedly presiding over their activities was a familiar Sigma Chi face. I waved but got no response.

"How quickly they forget" was barely out of my mouth when the Sigma Chi face caught sight of Mark and broadened into a dazzling smile. Mark had obviously made a more favorable impression than I had.

"You rushed Sigma Chi too?" I asked him.

"Yeah, doesn't everybody?" answered Mark wistfully as the distant face turned to bark orders to the pledges on their side of the hedge.

"Yeah, sort of. But Eddie," I said, nodding to the drill sergeant, "was the only guy I really liked."

"I should go thank him for the bid," Mark said. "He was nice."

I was right — Mark had made more of an impression. He had received a formal invitation to join Sigma Chi, and I hadn't. I checked the sky to see if the sun had gone behind a cloud. "Yeah," I sighed. "He's probably not too pleased that he lost you to this dump."

"And he lost you too," Mark grinned.

"Well, not really. I didn't—"

"Get to work, butt holes!" exploded from our kitchen window.

"Maybe I did pledge the wrong house," Mark grumbled.

"No way," I said, nipping this line of reasoning in the bud by pitching my new best friend a burlap sack. "Sigma Chi is so predictable. Too many blond boys with too much of daddy's money."

"Yeah," Mark pondered, "what did they see in us, anyway?"

"Beats me," I said, but I knew what they saw in Mark. "Maybe variety." I smiled.

"Well, we found variety," Mark chuckled, turning to our fraternity house. "This place is a zoo."

He had a point. Our bastion of brotherhood was, if nothing else, diverse. One common denominator bound this unlikely group of thirty-seven young men to a common purpose: the unyielding pursuit of hedonism. Not that this ideal was missing in other fraternities, but qualities such as brains, good looks, or social responsibility dulled their passion for pure decadence. Though as I recall, Mark was a compilation of all of the above, especially the good looks.

"Why did you pledge here?" I asked, my curiosity obliterating my better judgment. Mark could "fit in" at Sigma Chi or anywhere else.

"One night I got wasted here and committed."

Committing was an oath of intent.

"They can't hold you to that if you're wasted." My sense of fair play escaped in spite of my anxiety that Mark might end up rethinking his decision. I must have sounded indignant.

"Sure they can. Hey, no big deal, buddy," Mark said calmly, putting a comforting hand on my shoulder.

I felt the autumn sun shine a little brighter.

"So, you going out for intramurals?" he asked me.

"Maybe football," I said, sounding almost apologetic. "I have a bad shoulder from high school."

"What position?"

"Bench-warming quarterback."

"How'd you hurt your shoulder?"

"How didn't I?"

"Well, I played tight end and wide receiver. We're a team."

And what a tight end. Shaking the image from my head, I returned to our earlier unresolved conversation. "So," I said, "you don't really want to be a Sigma Chi?" Now *I* wanted a commitment.

"Naw. You saw the movie *Animal House,* didn't you?"

"Toga, toga, toga!"

"Right. And we are there," he said, extending his arms as if presenting our fraternity house in a brand new light. "Besides, you're my only competition. If we work it right, any babe that walks through that door will be yours or mine…or ours."

He winked. I blushed. He was joking, wasn't he? I suddenly didn't care about the "babes."

"I always believe in cooperation," I managed awkwardly.

"Then we'll do just fine, bud. What I can't figure out is how we could rush the same two dens of iniquity for eight full weeks and not run into each other."

I shrugged. I usually blanked on names but not on faces...not faces like Mark's.

From the front door another demented brother yelled at us: "Get to work, dick brains!"

"Climb on and rotate, fuckface!" Mark yelled back, his middle finger shot high in defiance.

Suddenly Mark lunged at me and wrestled me to the ground in the pile of golden leaves. I was so surprised, I didn't put up much resistance. Then, just as suddenly, he jumped up and yelled, "It's us against them!"

Mark charged the house, laughing like a crazy man and chasing the smaller, offending brother inside. I sat for a moment, savoring the smell of the decaying leaves, the smoke from a neighboring chimney, and the afternoon when I met Mark. I looked at Sigma Chi and thought that their loss was my gain.

By our second year, this time as full-fledged brothers, Mark and I shared an attic bedroom in the fraternity house, and our dates never saw the downstairs area if we could help it. We were hell-bent on scoring and had a reputation to uphold. Mark and I did attract the best-looking girls that ventured into our fraternal lunatic asylum, and with his looks and my enthusiasm, we made a formidable pair of heartbreakers...but my heart was never really in it.

We "borrowed" a DO NOT DISTURB sign from the local Howard Johnson's Motor Lodge that we hung on the door for only one purpose: "Sex in progress – go away." I had suppressed my feelings for Mark, but I always felt a stab of jealousy when the sign was up...and I was on the outside.

There were a few times when our dates stayed overnight, so we erected a makeshift partition between our twin beds: a sheet pinned to a clothesline that was nailed to opposing walls. not very decorative, but quite functional. The partition could not, however, muffle Mark's moans and sighs, making these late-night sexual experiences more vicarious than personal. I closed my eyes and imagined Mark and the object of his lust on the other side of the thin sheet.

As the semester progressed, there were fewer "dates," as Mark went over to Sigma Chi and took off for parts unknown with his friend Eddie. I was never invited and felt hurt, but Mark always made it up to me just by being a good friend. But by now I knew I was painfully in love and sublimating only with enormous effort. The bad karma I had accumulated by using really nice girls for my selfish pleasure was justly coming back to take revenge.

Then one day Eddie was no longer Mark's friend, and Mark didn't want to discuss it. At the time I was confused but privately overjoyed. Mark didn't seem particularly upset and started dating again with a vengeance – never the same girl twice. I, on the other hand, poured myself into my studies, to which my parents had so generously contributed tuition and expectations.

On the way to the library a few weeks later, I realized I'd forgotten to bring a book that desperately needed returning. I doubled back and ran into the house and up the stairs. The bedroom door was closed, but the DO NOT DISTURB sign was not on display, so I popped in to get my book.

"Jesus! Can't you knock?"

I was speechless. There stood Mark, stark naked in front of a full-length mirror, in front of which he had obviously been beating off. He didn't even try to cover up his erection.

"Shut the door, for Chrissakes," he said.

"I'm...I'm sorry," I stammered. "You should have put the sign..." I couldn't finish the sentence, and I couldn't take my eyes off Mark – and he knew it.

"You like?" Mark teased, strutting his tight ass around the room and playing with his hard-on. He was enjoying this, and I was dumbstruck. I was bursting at the seams – and he knew it! I was near tears when Mark stopped. He quietly hung the DO NOT DISTURB sign outside, then closed and locked the door.

"Come here, Steve," Mark said seriously, his erection losing some of its attitude. He held out his hand, and I took it.

"Put your notebook on the desk, Steve."

I did.

"Now take off your clothes, Steve."

I did.

Mark then took me in his arms and kissed me like I had never been kissed before, and I kissed back. His sandpaper face and solid body toppled my inhibitions like a flying body block. He paused.

"Can you talk now, Steve?"

"What can I say?"

"Yeah, well, I can see that your dick says it all," Mark said, stroking me till my knees almost buckled. "Damn, it's bigger than I thought it would be. But don't come yet! I want to show you everything I've wanted to show you since the day we met."

"What took you so long, damn it?" I blurted out. "I've been living in hell." My head was spinning.

"You were so uptight, I wasn't sure. You never gave me a clue."

"I don't want other guys, but..."

"But what?"

"But...am I a substitute?"

"For what?"

"You know, like, am I pinch-hitting...for a 'babe'...or for...'the Sweetheart of Sigma Chi'?"

"You knew about Eddie and me?"

"I do now." I finally smiled.

"Yeah, well, that's over. All of it."

"All of it?" I said cupping his incredible ass with my eager hands.

Instead of answering, Mark pulled away, sauntered over to the partition, and ripped the sheet off the clothesline. He bundled it up and tossed it into the trash can. Returning, he pulled me into his bed and kissed me with uncharacteristic tenderness. He then proceeded to run his tongue down my torso and take my cock in his mouth just before it exploded. After finishing me off, Mark looked up with those beautiful eyes and asked, "Does that answer your question?"

It answered all of my questions.

A WEEKEND THAT LASTED FOREVER

by Walter R. Ruzycki

In 1954 I lived on Jones Street in San Francisco, across the street from Grace Cathedral on Nob Hill. I had a one-room furnished apartment. The couch converted into a bed at night.

I was working for the Southern Pacific Railroad Company in the passenger department. The office was in the Southern Pacific building on Market Street, and there was a big SP sign on the roof. So many of the employees were gay, the joke in San Francisco was that the SP stood for "Swish Palace."

My job in the early morning was to contact interchange points in the SP system. I would find out what VIPs were on which trains so that appropriate arrangements could be made to greet them at their destinations. Ted worked for Southern Pacific's Los Angeles office, and he lived in Long Beach. We had never met each other, but he was my contact in Los Angeles. We spoke to each other almost every day on the telephone.

One day in January 1955, he asked if I had done anything exciting over the weekend. I told him it had been my birthday and that I had celebrated by buying and eating a bag of peanuts. I had been in San Francisco only about six months and didn't have any friends yet. Ted said he was sorry about that and that he wanted to come and meet me and throw me a proper birthday party. I was reluctant but said OK, I'd meet him at my apartment. He arrived on February fifth, planning on staying three days.

I wasn't sure Ted was gay, but I suspected. And I had no idea what he looked like. When he came to my apartment, I opened the door, we looked at each other, said hello, and kissed. My hunch had been right.

Ted had been in San Francisco fourteen years earlier, just before the war, when he was in the Army and stationed at the Presidio prior to being shipped out to Australia. I had been stationed at Camp Stoneman near Antioch, in 1948. I had visited San Francisco but didn't know it well. Ted knew even less about the city because his unit was often on alert and he had to stay close by the Presidio. But on that weekend when he came to visit me in February 1955, we eventually had to go looking for a restaurant.

We went walking down Powell Street. At the corner of Powell and Post streets was a drugstore. Across the street was Roos Brothers Men's Wear, which later became Roos Atkins. Ted had told me he didn't know anyone in San Francisco, but as we passed the drugstore, a man came walking out and shouted at Ted. At the same time, Ted shouted at the man. Then they threw their arms around each other and kissed. In 1955 two men did not hug and kiss in public in San Francisco.

I kept walking down Powell Street thinking what a liar Ted was. He had said he didn't know anyone in San Francisco. Was he hugging and kissing a stranger? I didn't want anything to do with him any longer. I decided that when we got back to my apartment, I would tell him to pack up and leave and go back to Los Angeles.

Ted caught up with me and introduced me to Bob. Ted and Bob had known each other in Long Beach. Bob had been born in San Francisco, into one of the city's most prominent families, and the company he worked for transferred him to Los Angeles. But Bob didn't like it there and had transferred back to San Francisco. Neither Ted nor Bob knew the other was in town. I don't remember where the three of us went to dinner, but I do remember becoming good friends.

On February eighth Ted took the train back to Los Angeles. I didn't know until later that when he went back to work, he gave his boss thirty days' notice. He wrote me love letters, in green ink, every other day. He said he was coming back to San Francisco so that we could live together forever. I thought he was talking nonsense.

Meanwhile, he put all his household goods in storage in Long Beach. On March 5, 1955, he came back to San Francisco and moved in with me in my one-room apartment. We shared our love and lives together for the next thirty-eight years.

But, I might add, not in the same one-room apartment.

THE BRIDGE OF SAN FRANCISCO COUNTY

by Tom Musbach

Strolling on the Golden Gate Bridge is romantic, but jogging across it among hundreds of men and women with balloons tied to their wrists is a different experience. Such a colorful spectacle nevertheless began the romance of my life.

I was participating in the Balloons Over the Bay Run, an annual spring rite sponsored by the San Francisco FrontRunners. It was only my second outing with the gay and lesbian group, and I had come out as a gay man only months before. I wasn't looking for love, exactly, just for gay friends who were also runners.

I enjoyed the run on that beautiful morning in 1993. The views of the bay and city were stunning, and many fellow runners were also pleasing to the eye. Several looked like guys I wished to befriend, and I hoped that at least one of them would talk to me after the run.

I finished in the first wave of joggers, so I had to wait for the others before proceeding to the follow-up brunch.

People started gathering in small groups in the parking lot, while I stood alone, not knowing anybody. I felt I was the only newcomer. To calm my rising self-consciousness and insecurity, I busied myself with stretching, hoping to give the impression that I was a very serious athlete with no time to talk.

I was so busy looking busy that I didn't notice a dark-haired man approach me.

"Did you go to Brown?" he asked.

I was wearing a Brown University T-shirt, but I told him that I had not attended the school. He then asked me if I was a visitor to San Francisco, to which I also replied "No," adding that I had lived in the city for a year. I quickly realized that this was becoming an actual conversation, so I stopped feigning indifference. The man speaking to me was clean-cut and very physically fit — biceps and pecs to die for. He flashed a big smile as he talked, and his voice was a clear, masculine baritone. The voice alone gave me gut-fluttering thrills, so I shifted into question mode in order to keep him talking.

Soon we were back to the topic of college. He had attended Bowdoin College before receiving an MBA from Dartmouth. Not only was he cute, he was intelligent. He still had a trace of that New England formal charm — a quality I had admired in fellow Yale students a few years earlier. Perhaps he could be more than a friend. His name was Peter.

During brunch my mind raced through checklists of desired "Mr. Right" qualities. Intelligent, self-confident, good conversationalist, wholesome, and handsome — he scored well according to my standards. He had moved into the "potential boyfriend" zone. Then I overheard him say he was going later that night to the Naked Tribal Heat dance. Suddenly his wholesome rating dipped. I had seen posters of a beefy nude man advertising the dance, which I had assumed would be very sleazy. Too bad such an attractive, intelligent man was attending such a sordid occasion, I thought. His looks and muscles would make him very popular.

His age was the next revelation — ten years my senior. I had never considered dating someone that much older. His profile dropped further below my extremely picky standards. Suddenly I feared the worst: Maybe he was more interested in me than I was in him. At the same time, I wondered if he considered me — a far less muscular specimen — not his type, thus I was deluding myself into thinking he might ask me out.

The result was inner chaos. I had never had a boyfriend before, so I had no idea what to make of our interaction. I just knew that I did not want him to ask me out — that seemed like too much pressure to define "us" too soon. I needed more time and more data. Furthermore, he knew very little about my inexperience.

While driving me home, he remarked that it must have been easy for me to be "out" in Yale's progressive environment. I took a deep breath and told him that I was not out at Yale; I had come out only a few months before. Rather than lose interest in me, as I had feared, he cheerfully welcomed me to the gay community. He acted as though he had discovered it was my birthday.

Though I enjoyed his company, I dreaded the moment of our departure: Would he try to give me his phone number? Would he ask me out before I left his car? Such prospects seemed more than my obsessive, cautious, and melodramatic sensibilities could take at that moment.

Outside my apartment building, I decided to be businesslike: I offered him my hand to shake. I thanked him for the ride and for going out of his way to talk to me. He quickly pulled a small piece of paper and pen from the glove compartment and wrote his name on it. *Oh no, not the phone number,* I thought, trying to think of a tactful way of being indecisive.

After writing his name, he handed me the pen and paper, asking me to write my name. After I handed it back, he ripped the slip in half, giving me the half with his name. He said the half sheets would help us remember each other's names at the next FrontRunners event. I got out of the car and watched him drive away.

His simple gesture of exchanging only names turned him into Prince Charming. He didn't attempt any pick-up, nor did he force me to decide whether I wanted to see him again. He was secure enough to leave the possibilities open-ended, which was exactly what I needed. (Maybe I'm just inexperienced, but I need more than one meeting before taking the risk of going out with a man.) My concerns about his character and his age vanished, and I could not stop thinking about him for the rest of the day. Within a week I was hoping he would look me up in the phone book. Peter was definitely a man I wanted to get to know better.

And I did. The annual balloon-wearing run across the Golden Gate Bridge is now our anniversary ritual.

COMMUNE INTERESTS
by Robert Mahoney

I t was an unusual beginning and hasn't really ended. We live 1,800 miles apart now but talk on the phone once or twice a month and always end with, "Love you."

We met at Clearhouse, a ramshackle farmhouse in the midst of a derelict orchard, with a stream bisecting the horseshoe pit. Clearhouse was a haven for free spirits — some gay, more not — who gathered on weekends in groups of ten or fifteen to drink beer, smoke pot, barbeque, recite poetry, listen to endless tapes of the Grateful Dead, reflect on the ills of the larger society, and lament the recent passing of the hippie era that emancipated us. Clearhouse was not a commercial venture but a homestead with the atmosphere of a commune.

I was fifty, less ravaged than many when they reach that milestone, and still teaching then. He was eighteen, a student in an alternative high school and living away from home. It was his first visit to Clearhouse (he'd arrived with others I knew only vaguely,) and he seemed intimidated by the energy and content of the central dialogue, which focused on political and philosophical issues beyond his scope. Curious about the attractive boy and sensing his discomfort, I excused myself from the conversation and invited him to accompany me on a beer run, confident that my elderly right-drive Jaguar would spark his interest and give us something to talk about. I made no declaration during the thirty-minute round trip but attempted to reveal myself through innuendo, to which he did not directly respond — though his fondling of the Jag's gearshift appeared more than an unconscious gesture.

The boy was my opponent in horseshoes and partner at the pool table, but for the most part we circulated in different groups during the long Clearhouse day, our eyes meeting from time to time. I knew what mine were saying but was uncertain about his.

The rule at Clearhouse was, you slept where you fell, and if you happened to collapse in an empty bed, that was a bonus. I crashed a little before midnight — early for Clearhouse — and it must have been about four hours later when I awoke to find the boy fast asleep, deliciously nude, and snuggled up against me like a puppy. I put my arm around him — gently, so as not to disturb — and resumed my slumber, warmer now on that cold November night. Later that morning we made love, quietly and without preamble. His first comment afterward was, "I'm hungry."

I never in so many words asked him to move in with me, and the way he did it was subtle and charming. At first he'd visit a day or two at a time, then three with a change of clothes, then four or five with a laundry bag. I began to notice unfamiliar shoes and boots vying with mine for space. One day when I complained that my closet was overflowing, he grinned and said, "I guess we'll have to get a bigger place." It was a done deal.

THE DAY WE MET

I'd been married twice but had no children and had never shared my household with another man. Now I had not only a live-in lover but a surrogate son. I felt better about the disparity in our ages when he exchanged his high school books for college texts.

We were together thirteen years.

GLEEFUL CLUB
by Brian

He was minister of music at a church in Southern California. A choir member had been pestering him to invite a glee club from CalTech to come down for a concert. CalTech, a noted science and engineering school, does not conjure up thoughts of fine musicality. Finally, after the head pastor was pulled into the discussion, the minister relented and figured that the church might as well get some good out of it. The church choir would host the glee club as an activity for dinner and a Saturday concert; the glee club would stay overnight and sing for the church service in the morning, giving the regular choir a Sunday off.

That Saturday, the minister was in the church kitchen helping get the dinner together when he was informed that the glee club had arrived and was setting up in the sanctuary. He went to greet the visiting club and found two surprises.

He had entered the hall from the back, behind the risers the glee club had set up and was practicing on. First, he noticed, the glee club was good; second, there was this cute butt in tight white shorts and a mesh shirt standing at the top corner of the risers. He walked around, and he found that the front was better — tall, dark-haired, and handsome.

It was May 1983, and I was a grad student in engineering at CalTech and sang in the men's glee club. I had only been out since November 1982 and had only been dating since January. I had so little gaydar that it took the cruise of death to make me notice. I was dating a nice guy in L.A., but we were beginning to realize that it wasn't passion, just affection. After spending Saturday in my lab, I was grateful for the chance to get away, go sing, charm some nice church ladies, and read a good science-fiction novel.

As we rehearsed, the minister (who introduced himself as John) came in and welcomed us. I really didn't take much notice then; but later he "happened" to be in the dinner line next to me, and after we got our food, he sat next to me. As we talked through dinner, I thought that he was nice, interesting, and witty. He was good-looking too: a bearded redhead with green eyes and a sparkling smile.

I liked him immediately but was oblivious until we had finished. He excused himself, putting his hand on my shoulder as he said to the table of people, "Have a good concert." Somehow, in that touch, I had to suddenly reevaluate the previous hour. *Could he be interested?* I remember thinking. *A minister at a regular church?*

In my tuxedo, onstage for the concert, I would sneak glances at him and catch him looking at me and smiling. It was both distracting and exciting, but I needed to focus on the music.

I should digress here and explain that the older members of the glee club (those of legal drinking age) had a habit of going out barhopping and singing after our concerts. For this trip most of the group had brought sleeping bags to stay over at a church member's house after carousing — but they had neglected to inform me. Therefore, the glee club president had pulled my name from the list of people to be housed. After the concert I found out about all this and complained — and up popped John to offer a spare bed at his place. With heart in my mouth, I agreed. It was only later that I found out that John had been wondering how to get me reassigned ("Oh, I'll take this one!") but hadn't found me on the list.

John and a friend, Dennis, accompanied us out to several bars, where we drank and sang barbershop and Hawaiian folk songs and generally made an attractive nuisance of ourselves. John and I talked about music, science, religion, and a myriad other topics I can't recall. I do remember his sea-green eyes and discovering that he was a truly good person. John remembers that at one bar Dennis asked a CalTech friend of mine (the club president) about me.

"Oh, he's going through a rough time now. He broke up with his girlfriend of three years and still isn't over it," my friend replied.

Dennis began to use sign language to tell John, *He's straight!*

I don't think so, John signed back. Still, John began wondering if he was wrong. Could he be throwing a lot away over a sudden infatuation with this guy?

When we left that bar, I felt I needed to confirm what was going on, so I mentioned that I liked to dance at a famous gay disco in L.A. John asked if I wanted to go dancing at a gay disco in Laguna Beach. I became flustered but agreed.

The place was called the BoomBoom Room, and once we arrived, we got drinks and started dancing. The club was hot, so soon our shirts were off, my six-foot two-inch frame wrapped around his fuzzy five-foot nine-inch body. We danced over an hour, till I was about to burst my zipper.

On the way home he asked if I wanted to sleep in the spare bed or with him. After that hour on the dance floor, it seemed silly not to sleep together, but it was 3 a.m., and we had to be up at 7. So, as responsible adults, we agreed just to cuddle and sleep. Think again! The touch of him near me kept me aroused, awake, and crazy — and my arousal kept him the same. Finally, about 4 a.m., we gave up our good intentions and made love quickly and safely, putting us out of our misery.

After a few hours' sleep, we showered, ate breakfast, and got ready for church. He took a photo of me that morning at breakfast (grinning and puppy-eyed) that is still on his desk. After the morning service, we went to lunch together, exchanged phone numbers, and made plans to get together in a few days.

I drove back to Pasadena not quite believing what had happened, not knowing whether this was love or lust. I did know, however, that he was someone I wanted to see more of — and soon.

Over the years, we have learned to tell this story together — enjoying the irony that despite our belief in taking things slow, dating, and not rushing sex, we broke all these guidelines for each other.

NILE CRUISE

by James Russell Mayes

For several weeks after I arrived in Cairo, I would sit under a massive flame tree in front of my building, enjoying the breeze off the Nile and hoping to meet a friend. Amer worked nearby. He had a lovely, generous smile; a quick laugh; and honey-colored eyes. *He looks interesting,* I said to myself. I found myself staring at him a lot, and I noticed him looking at me too. He tried to introduce himself, but he spoke no English. I spoke no Arabic, and I could barely pronounce his name, which means "moon." We simply sat together among the other men in the street who became my friends and were teaching me the language. I had tea with them every night under the flame tree. They taught me by means of jokes, cursing one another, calling one another names, and acting out the meaning. Amer was the only one who did not tease me for using a dictionary. He took the time to make me understand things that the others had no patience for. Naturally, he became my favorite teacher.

We held hands in the dark and walked arm in arm up the street. These are not unusual activities for Egyptians who are close friends. It is custom, for example, to greet one another with a kiss on each cheek. Amer and I did so. We sailed the Nile, shared flowers and music and chocolate, watched bats fly past the palm trees at night. My Arabic got a lot of compliments.

As our affection for each other became more particular, the greeting changed: Our lips met so long as no one else was around to tease us. We grew secretive. We discovered things about each other, including sex, which occurred suddenly one night and without my wanting it to. I had decided for myself that I did not want to sacrifice such a meaningful friendship for anything. Then Amer misinterpreted an innocent hug. My guard was down.

The next day he was frozen with shame, afraid to speak to me. I apologized. I told him it was nothing. Friendship was more important. We would forget about sex. "Impossible," he said.

Strangely, we talked about God. Religion was not a pressing issue for me when I came to Egypt, but I never felt more of a Christian than I have here. To a Muslim I can say I believe in God without aligning myself with that repulsive fundamentalism that has infected religion, both his and mine. "Christians say that God is love," I told Amer. With his knowledge of the Koran and my knowledge of the Bible, we compared notes. We demanded responsibility for our beliefs.

Our next important conversation occurred when I asked Amer if he was ever going to get married. Lots of Egyptian men have sex with other men. But nearly all of them get married to women, eventually. It's the culture. Amer answered affirmatively, that he was planning to marry. That disappointed me. I asked him when. He answered with a question, which I've always though was a fair tactic: "How long are you going to live in Egypt?"

"I don't know, Amer," I replied. "Two years, maybe four, maybe eight."

"I will get married after eight years. In eight years you will be in America." He changed the subject. "Why aren't you married, Mr. Jim?"

"I don't want to be married," I said.

"Why? Marriage is good!"

I took a minute to think before I dropped the bomb. I told him, "I don't want a woman."

"In America," he asked, "is it possible for two men to marry?"

"Yes," I said, "there are some who do." I didn't have the words to explain that such a marriage is not legally recognized by our government.

"Do you want to marry a man?" he asked.

If any other Egyptian friend, including the ones I had slept with, had asked me that question, I would have lied. To Amer I said, "Maybe." Then I admitted it: "Yes."

"Who?"

The question surprised me. Amer probably knew the answer before I did. I was not thinking where the conversation was going when it started out. I only wanted to know, in the midst of my loneliness, if there were such a thing, if it were possible, in spite of what I had been told by nearly everyone, for there to be *one* Egyptian man who loved men only, a man who loved another man so much that he might not marry a woman at all. "You," I said.

"Oh, Mr. Jim!" He was instantly extraordinarily happy. I was embarrassed for him. "Yes! Yes! I will marry you!"

"Wait," I said. "We need to think about this…"

"When I go home this weekend, I will think. I will give you my answer."

THE DAY WE MET

I don't know whether I was afraid that he would say yes or that he'd say no. Before he left I hauled him into the shadows of the garage under my building, the place where we usually did our kissing. I shared my doubts about the differences in our cultures, languages, and religions. I told him, after we heartily agreed that we loved each other very much, that we had all the time in the world. We could wait for the whole time I was in Egypt and *then* decide whether we wanted to.

But Amer is brave. He went home for his holiday. He mooned around the house. He slept late and a lot, so much so that his mother asked him what was wrong. He told her that he missed his sweetheart, Mr. Jim. He told me all of this when he came back to Cairo. "I will marry you," he told me on his return. I brought up our differences again. "So American!" Amer said. "If there is love, there is no problem. Love does not know Egyptian or American. Love does not know Christian or Muslim, man or woman. This is love. Love is from God."

I was ecstatic. It is a powerful mystery that two men can love each other and that love can mean so much that they will sacrifice their traditions, public approval, and perhaps even the laws of their respective governments for it.

A BELIEVER

by Brian Moore

Of all the places one would expect to meet a lover and life partner, church probably ranks near the bottom of the list. But when the initial meeting takes place at a Roman Catholic parish church during a charismatic prayer meeting, I think it becomes news.

I was thirty-two years old and not totally out of the closet, using religion as a camouflage and smoke screen. A gay friend of mine, Mark, also attended the prayer meetings, and when he came out to me, I had no real choice but to come out in return. An eighteen-year-old named Rob started attending the prayer meetings, and Mark and I speculated that he had to be gay. My mother even made the assumption. Mark seized the moment just prior to leaving for college. Mark told me all the details, but he also said that he didn't love Rob and that maybe I would want to take him under my wing.

I approached Rob at the first prayer meeting after Mark had left. I simply told him that we had something special in common and that if he ever needed to talk to anyone, he could call me. Rob waited exactly ten days to call and invite me on a date.

We went to a movie and then to dinner. I tried to explain to Rob that being gay was nothing to be ashamed of but that it was something he could not share at the prayer meetings. Dinner seemed to take forever, and I later realized that he was stalling for time. When we got back in my car, he acted very nervous. Finally he said that if we drove around for another half hour, we could go back to his apartment because his mother worked the night shift as a nurse. I made him feel more comfortable by responding that I thought he would never ask. And that was the truth.

The rest of that evening is a blur, but I know that I broke one of my rules: We had sex on the first date — but even Rob will admit that I was the one seduced.

This first attempt at a relationship lasted for about nine months. Rob would call on Saturday nights and tell me the "coast was clear" and that we would have the apartment to ourselves. He always greeted me at the door with some fantastically erotic theme (jock, construction worker, businessman in a suit without trousers, or totally *au naturel*). My affection for him was growing, and I realized that I needed to give him some of the positive gay experiences so many of us had lacked as adolescents.

I took him to Dignity and introduced him to Catholics who were living with integrity as gay Christians. We also went to the theater and to private parties. However, the smartest move I made was to take him to the Metropolitan Community Church, the predominantly gay and lesbian church in our area. I rationalized that if he ever became totally disillusioned with other religions, he might remember this as a place to return to fortify his faith in himself as a gay Christian.

But in the end Rob decided that he was too young to commit to a relationship, and he disappeared from my life. There were several very brief and feeble attempts at communication during the next ten years, but I was never able to find him. His closest friend told me that over the years, Rob had toyed with the idea of trying to find me.

During a bad period in my life — when I was unemployed and depressed and fairly disenchanted with the Roman Catholic Church following papal statements calling us "intrinsically evil" and worse — I attended a Metropolitan Community Church service with my mother. A very scruffy-looking young man was in attendance. It was Rob, but we didn't recognize each other. My mother and I went back to the church the following week, and this same young man was sitting several rows in front of us. As they passed the attendance board, I saw his name and almost had heart failure. I didn't know what to do.

After the service I approached him and started to say, "I have no reason to expect that you remember me, but—" and he immediately threw his arms around me. Let's just say it was a very emotional reunion. As we departed neither of us had any idea what was going to happen next. I wanted to believe it was "divine intervention" again.

We took things slowly, making no commitments, and we certainly did not jump into bed. He had also told me from the outset that he was HIV-positive, and I could honestly say that I didn't care. I had never stopped loving him during those years in between, and I was not going to reject him during the hopefully good years we would have ahead of us.

The slow and cautious approach lasted for about three months. I then invited him to take a Circle Line cruise around Manhattan, have dinner at a posh restaurant, and see a play. The turning point came on the boat ride. He put his head on my shoulder, and without hesitation I put my arm around him; we looked like any other couple in love. This was Manhattan, and if people stared at us, they quickly looked away and found something else to look at. In my mind I had to let Rob know I loved him unconditionally and didn't care if that meant letting the whole world in on the "secret."

Three weeks later, after a church service, we went to dinner and he started to grab my hand under the table. I didn't know what he was doing and was a little embarrassed. He was trying to slip a ring on my finger and panicked when he thought I was rejecting it. I quickly came to my senses and slipped a ring from my hand onto his finger. Neither one of us has any recollection of what we had for dinner at that Italian restaurant that night.

Almost five years later Rob is not only my lover but my best friend. He is not the kid I had first met years before. He is extremely bright, has a fantastic sense of humor, and shows a love and caring that always makes me feel that my love is returned. People tell me that I glow when I talk about him, and I've heard many times that he reacts the same way when talking about me.

I thank God for bringing us together twice, because I just don't believe that this was a coincidence. It may have been a lesson that has taught me to appreciate Rob more because he really is a twice-given gift.

NEVER ALONE

by Michael D. Headings

Rick and I had been friends for a number of years. It was the one good thing to come out of a poor summer relationship that ended on a rather sour note. The two of us had a lot of fun — purely platonic, but with a slight edge to it. I guess if I had been willing, there could have been more. I was not willing.

Rick and I had gotten together over the past couple of years to spend time with each other, laughing and forgetting the sometimes mundane routines of life. Many of our "scandalous adventures," as they came to be known, had us spending long weekends at Delaware's Rehoboth Beach. Rick, always the center of attention, usually sat on the beach with a small hand-held mirror to flash the sun into the face of some unsuspecting gorgeous Speedo-clad man. Instantly he turned on his charm, and we had one more person to join in on the laughter and fun. Many days we'd end up with five or six guys sitting with us. Such was Rick's personality and attraction. He was not promiscuous, nor did he pressure anyone. He was simply playful, and people felt safe and happy in his presence.

I was then thirty-one years old and very weary of the bar scene. I had not met anyone with whom I remotely thought I would end up spending my life. Not that I hadn't tried. I was slowly coming to the sad realization that maybe I would spend the rest of my years alone. I had wanted somebody in my life for as long as I could remember, but the prospects of that happening, I thought, were slim at best.

The last summer that Rick and I made our annual pilgrimage, Rick had been late getting down to the bed and breakfast. A message from him was waiting for me when I arrived, telling me to go to the beach without him. He would try to make it down about 5 or 6 o'clock.

Flying solo, I took off for the beach ready for some relaxation. Poodle Beach, as it is affectionately known, is at the upper end of Rehoboth. I made the long trek to the beach and found a spot in the sand that I claimed for myself.

As the day wore on, the sky began to show a few gray clouds. I didn't think much of it at the time and continued to bask in the warm summer sun. I was tired and began to doze a little, waking up about forty-five minutes later to more darkening clouds. I noticed a few people packing to leave. Being a die-hard beach fan, I was determined to stay until I was kicked off. So I started to check out the scenery. Off to the back of the beach was somebody I hadn't seen before. He was good-looking, at least from my vantage point, and he lay on his towel alone.

I found myself staring until I noticed that he had looked up and was now staring directly back at me. Not wanting it to appear as if I were ogling, I turned and looked elsewhere. Typical of gay fashion, I was just biding my time until I felt I could steal another glance. Sure enough, when I did, he shot another glance my way.

A small cloud then began to spit rain. Within an instant several hundred beach queens shot up and let out a small scream of panic in unison, as if it had been rehearsed to take place on cue. I sat there chuckling to myself as everyone on my end of the beach quickly packed and left. I couldn't help thinking of the scene in *The Wizard of Oz* when the wicked witch gets wet, screams, and melts. I knew this would be a short-lived drizzle, though, so I stood my ground. As the mass exodus neared completion, I noticed the guy that had caught my eye earlier also standing his ground. We caught eyes again and smiled, but neither of us made the motion to move.

The sun did come back out, but only for about ten minutes. Then another series of dark clouds began to approach, this time with lightning. The clear-the-beach signal was given, and the rest of us were forced to pack up and go. I gathered my things and purposely strolled by the guy I had been drooling over since I set eyes on him. We exchanged smiles and made benign small talk for a few minutes, after which we parted and I walked back to the bed and breakfast. I figured I would probably not see him again, and I thought trying to hook up with someone down there would have been ridiculous, as he probably lived too far from me to see each other regularly anyway. How's that for a jaded thought process?

When I got back to the bed and breakfast, I sat on the back porch chatting with another guest. Our conversation paused, however, when the door to the back porch opened and the guy from the beach stepped through to get to the outside showers. I couldn't believe it.

The next day, while I was taking my shower and getting ready to go out, Rick, who finally rolled into town the night before, met the guy I had spied on the beach. His name, Rick found out, was Joseph.

The next morning, while Rick was getting ready, Joseph and I sat on the front porch and talked in depth for the first time. As it turned out, he was single and looking for a relationship, lived a few minutes outside Baltimore, and was sincere as well as deadly handsome. We briefly ran into each other on the beach and in the clubs that weekend and ended up giving each other business cards and home phone numbers. He called the following week, and we talked for a long time. He invited me down to his place for Labor Day weekend, and I accepted.

That weekend was the best I had had in a long time. From that point, we saw each other every weekend and spoke to each other every day. We fell in love and never stopped caring for each other. Less than a year later, we married and bought a house together in the Maryland countryside.

It still amazes me to this day that after all the hurt and the resignation of living single, of swearing off the bars, and of despising dates that were out for only one thing, that I had truly found what I desperately wanted in my heart. I found a soul mate who cares for me, helps me grow, and loves me as much as I love him.

A DIFFERENT KIND OF CONGREGATING

by Jesse G. Monteagudo

I met Michael at synagogue. We came together with vastly different experiences. It was Michael's first time there, and I was leading services. He had recently come out of the closet, whereas I had been actively involved in my community for more than a decade. He had never had a male lover before, while I was at the end of a nine-year, codependent relationship that existed in name only.

Congregation Etz Chaim, Miami's gay synagogue, did not have a rabbi, and services were led by a layperson. As a relatively knowledgeable member of my synagogue, I occasionally conducted them. I must admit that I was not in a religious frame of mind that February night. Having rejoined bachelorhood with a vengeance, I wanted to get the service over with so that I could head off to the baths. Michael, a professional musician, almost didn't make it himself. The Polish National Dance Company was playing in town that night, and Michael had to choose between attending their concert or going to temple. He chose the latter.

Though Michael and I half-heartedly met before services, he didn't register with me until after they had begun. That's when I noticed him, sitting in the back row, smiling at me. At first I didn't know what to make of it. Though I found him attractive enough, I had no intention of dating him, much less marrying him. Synagogue is for praying, not for cruising.

Afterward Michael came up to me, and we started talking. He told me about himself, his background, his interests, and his concerns about safer sex. I made a remark to the effect that safer sex could be fun, which he took to be a come-on (or so he told me later). There's no telling what might have happened that night had Michael not been invited to join a group at an all-night deli for late supper. Since I had already had dinner, I declined the invitation. Michael went off to eat, and I went to the baths.

The next Friday night, Michael tells me, he came back to the synagogue hoping to see me again. I wasn't there; I was in Orlando attending a run sponsored by a local Levi's-and-leather club. Michael was the last thing on my mind. I returned the following week only to find him still waiting for me and hoping to pick up where we had left off two weeks earlier.

We started talking, and I remembered what it was that had attracted me to him: his wit; his curiosity; his rich, dark beard; his bright eyes; and his bewitching smile. We went to a club, where we talked and danced, fast at first but then, the music to the contrary, slow. When we danced slow, the world disappeared. That's when Michael invited me to go home with him.

Though I did not wish to start a relationship at the time, Michael would not take no for an answer. Undaunted by the fact that I was still living with my ex, Michael kept after me, trusting that the feeling was mutual. It was. Michael went from being one of many to being the main one to being the only one. We officially became an item during the first weekend of May, which was also the weekend of Etz Chaim's anniversary and of my birthday. Several months later Michael and I moved in together, and what started as a smiling face at services turned into a relationship that is ten years old and still going strong.

THE THIRTY-DAY PLAN
by Lynn Jeffries

I had heard about Ben almost two years before we met. I was involved in a club for big men and the men who admire them. The club secretary, Tom, phoned one evening to read me an inquiry letter that the club had received from a twenty-year-old virgin who described the type of man he found interesting. I wondered whether someone had sent him my résumé and a nude photo, because he was describing me.

Still my life was in a space that couldn't let me give proper attention to a relationship, so Tom got together with Ben instead.

During the time they were getting acquainted, we never met. Then, almost immediately after, problems in the club caused me to resign and to end my friendship with Tom. For over a year he left messages on my answering machine and wrote letters trying to renew our friendship. In one letter he said he'd like to talk with me again and that Ben would enjoy looking at me.

The letter angered me. I am a big man, about 365 pounds and a very hairy, bearded "bear" type. But I'm not a hunk of hairy fat to be stared at. I'm also an intelligent, talented, highly educated person. I want to be seen as all of myself, not just as the object of someone's fetish.

Shortly after I received the letter, I was visiting my friend Carroll, who lived a few blocks from where Ben and Tom lived. He mentioned that Ben worked in a video store nearby, and I said, "Well, Tom says Ben would enjoy looking at me. Maybe we should give him a chance." We stopped to rent a couple of tapes, but Ben wasn't working that day.

On the way out of town the next night, I returned the videos alone, and Ben was behind the counter. When he saw the name of the customer on the account, he said, "Uh, tell Carroll I said hi. I know him." I said I would and, with a sudden attack of shyness, left.

The next night Carroll received a call from Tom. "Who the hell took back your videos?" he demanded. All Ben had told him, apparently, was that a gorgeous big bear had returned the tapes. Carroll told me later that he was sure Ben was interested in me.

Was it love at first sight? For me, it was certainly lust at first sight. I was attracted to his tall, thin body and the timid but warm smile he flashed my way. And he had the slightly receding hairline that's always made me melt. I also knew he was a writer, so we had a common interest. I told Carroll that I would have him in bed within thirty days and living with me in six months.

The next day, I found an excuse to get my car repaired in the area and called the video store. When Ben answered, I simply said, "Did anybody ever tell you you have a wonderful smile?" I had intended to tell him that it would look even better wrapped around my hard cock, but I chickened out at the last minute. When he recovered from a state of shock, he agreed that I could stay in the store with him while my car was being worked on.

For one entire afternoon we read my poems and a porn story in progress and got acquainted. We were both totally circumspect, but there was an obvious charge in the atmosphere. As I was getting out of his car to pick up mine, I asked if Tom knew we had spent the day together. Even though he told me Tom was fully aware, I told him I wanted to get together again and hoped that something might develop.

A couple of days later, a letter arrived with some of Ben's poems and enough comments about how much he'd enjoyed the day that I knew he wanted me too. I phoned to ask if we could spend his day off together the following week. Since I lived seventy miles away and didn't feel comfortable meeting at Tom's place, I offered to rent a cheap motel room where we could talk privately.

Then I sent him a long letter, in which I finally expressed my desire to make love to him. The story he'd read the first day we were together had a hot shower scene, and he told me he'd always had a shower fantasy. So I told him the room would have a shower and two beds. We could use those or sit in the chairs and discuss poetry — whatever he wanted. If he wanted the shower and bed, all he had to say was, "Let's."

The morning of our first real date, we met for breakfast, then went to the motel. We had to wait two hours for the motel's only set of sheets to dry, and Ben was obviously becoming more nervous by the minute. When we finally got into the room, I turned to lock the door. When I turned around again, I found Ben standing by one of the beds, trembling. He merely looked at me and nodded. As I took him in my arms and gently pushed him onto the bed, he said, "I really need a shower."

Before Tom was to get home from work, we'd fucked and sucked in just about every possible position, acting out more than one of Ben's fantasies. I was just a few days short of my forty-second birthday, and I hadn't had so many orgasms in such a brief period of time in nearly twenty years. Even more important, I'd never felt such peace as in his arms, and he told me he felt the same. We both tried to hold back the words, but we had fallen in love, and we told each other so.

The night I returned the videos was July twenty-fifth. We went to the motel August eighteenth. He moved in on Labor Day. We've now been together almost two years, and it gets better all the time. I've pledged to spend at least sixty years with him, if he can last that long.

SPOUSEY

by Chris Siegenhart

F ate follows a script all its own. I am convinced that there lies a good dose of rhyme and reason behind the collage of people, experiences, and coincidences we encounter and how we react.

Jimmy.

It wasn't so much guilt that made me join. It was more like a fear-inspired sense of obligation after my verdict came in negative. So I put my "One oughta do something" mumble into action.

I'm not much of a joiner, but the buddy group was different from the start. Basic training, basic sharing of emotions I had not yet unearthed. My first "client," Jimmy, quickly puts a human face over the four-letter disease. A very private person and lifelong negative thinker, Jimmy is far advanced already. Eventually, we are breaking through to each other, having some heart-to-hearts. Holding hands after he has become half blind and half demented. When he dies, after half a year, his eyes by this time totally blind, his mind totally gone, I wail uncontrollably, as I suddenly feel as if nobody cares — not society, not the governor, not Jimmy's family.

Me.

This kind of experience, I found, makes you look at yourself, makes you want to make a difference, change pace perhaps, have impact. Now, the need for impact is definitely not what attracted me to skydiving. Call it an early midlife crisis for a guy in his mid thirties. Breathtaking minutes of freefall through clear blue skies over New York certainly helped clear away my blues.

Back on the ground, Jimmy's sister and I sew a quilt for Jimmy, and I move on to a new "assignment."

George.

At first glance George is a tough and gruff former IV-drug user. Far from my hoped-for heroic Prince Charming who would, of course, sport blond locks, forever in place, and be open-minded enough for a two-way crush. What could possibly be wrong with some discreet romance, sweet, safe, and fabulous, in spite of it all? The potential for sad days ahead or Hollywood-teary moments does not enter the scenario in my foolish mind.

Washington, D.C.

I am in a long-distance relationship with a sweet guy from D.C., my first serious entanglement in many years. It is not just the three hundred miles that seems to keep us from growing closer or more serious.

David.

We have a buddy retreat at a splendid old farmhouse in December of '88. High ceilings, stone walls, fireplace. This is where I lay my eyes on this young man: tall, slender, serious, with a wonderful smile and an infectious roaring laugh, in tight 501s jeans, on the floor, his back to the fireplace, in a room full of volunteers and professionals. I catch his name in the introductions: David. He's a social-work student with the agency, an active, brainy participant in the discussion group. He does not register me. Too shy to take the initiative, I take him home instead, filing him in my imagination's romantic wing.

Us.

Months later I see you at the hot new dance place in our tame Westchester neighborhood. Inhibitions liberated by a few cuba libres, I walk up and shake your hand. "Hi, David," I say. "I know you from the AIDS group."

The wheels in your brain go into a mad spin. *Oh, boy, he's probably a client,* is your first hunch, which would put involvement in the no-no bracket. We chat. We hug. We kiss. We exchange numbers.

You call the next day. We make a date. You bring flowers. You floor me. I search for a vase. Nobody's ever brought me flowers before. What's this guy doing to me? We hit it off. No sex. Sorry. Let's stay monogamous, shall we?

I see D.C. A difficult talk. Tears. Over. Clean.

David and I become an item. Oh, does it feel right.

Me again.

I'm still this freewheeling bachelor spirit — never in terms of testosterone-laden escapades — but with my own untamed agenda and a certain to-fly-is-human notion, mandating long weekends at parachute drop zones.

It almost sounds like an ultimatum when, out of the blue, you ask me to take a turn onto a two-way street.

I tremble as I contemplate blowing it. Don't I have a right to be my own worst enemy?

Your concept of togetherness has its revolutionary appeal. I'm ripe for the taking, I slowly realize, half in fear, half in anticipation. Months after our first I love yous, we move in together, an all-time first for me.

Spouseys.

Amazing how little give-and-take it takes. It feels so right that we don't see the need for society to slap its stamp of approval onto our modestly limp wrists. But hey, why not? We're worth it and deserve it. We end up in a neat church with an open-arms ideology, a maverick minister, and a group of elders who initially turn their thumbs down on us, until they find a simple majority of heart months later and allow us to nervously walk down the aisle and vow our I dos.

And now suburbia has another blessed family of four — sheps included, a boy and a girl.

My buddy George comes over on occasion; he has come totally clean and proves to be way smarter than street-smart, with a heart of gold in a hard shell, defying odds and finding purpose for many years.

David and I are painfully aware of the sheer knock-down force of this violent surf that has been beating down on and around us. It has opened our hearts and minds too. It brought us together on that December day that stands out in my mind and is all fogged up in his.

Madly in love, snugly at peace — what a winning formula for a genuine fairy tale to end happily ever after.

SNOWBOUND
by David J. Weidman

ourteen inches of snow on the ground, and the sky looked as if a frustrated writer had attacked it with Wite-Out. My students at Kimball Union Academy were too polite to ask where their crazy teacher might be headed at 8 p.m. after his biweekly faculty meeting. I had dragged their sorry asses out of the dorm to help pull, push, and swear my gutless Honda Civic out of the inundated parking lot. I have never been so determined to make something happen.

Four years earlier I bought this silver machine, then sleek and proud, in order to make my wife mad with jealousy. She was divorcing me. Now after years of faithful service, I prayed to God that the car would see me through once again. As I skied down Route 120 at an even thirty miles per hour, balancing that crucial formula of not too fast and not too slow, desperately concentrating on staying in the preestablished ruts created by other desperadoes, I barely had time to reflect on the past several weeks.

Sick of allowing my puritanical upbringing and my conservative prep-school environment to keep me from a loving partnership, I had "taken the driver's seat of my life," as my missionary dad had instructed me to do many times over the years. (He's probably rolling over in his grave as he witnesses the application of his adage.) Losing thirty-five pounds in six weeks with a severe diet and workout program, I looked and felt the best that I could hope to be. Then I daringly placed a penny personal ad in *It's Classified.* Surprisingly for rural New Hampshire, over the past six months, it brought many responses to my post-office box. Now however, after two dozen attempts, I had grown tired of this seemingly endless dating game.

Where is Mr. Right? became my mantra. Three weeks earlier, with precious few personal moments to spare while directing the school's annual winter musical, I halfheartedly took my ritual journey, down the same lonely road I was now traveling, to that small, square mailbox that held my future happiness behind its red emblazoned #912. There was a solitary envelope.

After weeks of correspondence and communicating with answering machines, we finally agreed to meet at Lui Lui's in West Lebanon. Pizza and pasta, with a table separating us in case of the need to abort the mission. I was experienced.

As I miraculously arrived at the destination, one lonely car waited impatiently in the parking lot, headlights blazing like a beacon of hope.

Dutifully I walked to the restaurant door. It was locked. Closed early. My frozen heart burned as I sludged my way over to the dual rays.

"Hi...Tom?" He was cute. Trim. Invitingly dressed: L.L. Bean no-nonsense casual.

"Let's try Sweet Tomatoes," he offered. "They were open a few minutes ago."

"I'll follow you." If I knew then what I know now, the significance of those words would have left me completely paralyzed, frozen stiff.

I turned off the radio to concentrate further on the road. Even his brake lights seemed to beckon me.

Sweet Tomatoes's waiters were efficiently putting the chairs on the tables, eager to make it home before the storm made any movement impossible. We drove by. Now what? *Please, God,* I begged to myself, *don't let this not happen.*

Parking in the only available space, I came to a crunchy halt behind the Lebanon Opera House. Awkward pause. I watched Tom squint through the wind and estimate the chances of my being a lunatic ax murderer. We had corresponded. Several letters back and forth. Our busy work schedules prohibited an earlier meeting. It had been over three weeks — anticipation building the whole time. He knew I had been born and raised in India, growing up in the foothills of the Himalayan Mountains. I taught theater. I passed the test.

"Well, I just got back from a trip," he said. "There's not much in the cupboards, but you're welcome to come up to my place, and we'll find something to eat."

I sat on the drain board and watched him maneuver around the kitchen. He was obviously skilled. Flight attendants can work under pressure, especially if it involves service. I offered to help, but there wasn't really a lot to do.

Soon we found ourselves across from each other at his huge, sturdy dining table, the central attraction in his small living/dining room. The snow streaked down. Charlie Parker and the candles softened the rough edges of our uncertainties. Ragu never tasted so good.

Theater and travel, our similar passions, were central themes. Tom mesmerized me with story after hilarious story of his escapades as a flight attendant. He is fluent in

Spanish, so he flew the Caribbean routes. There was the Puerto Rican woman who wanted to have her child born on the mainland – and almost didn't make it. Another Puerto Rican family wanted to have their father buried in the homeland. After each member violently denied the flight attendants an opportunity to offer the elderly gentleman beverages or food, an attentive flight attendant noticed he hadn't moved for several hours, apparently comatose. Tom, who was in charge of that flight, approached a son and in Spanish pithily inquired, "Dead?" The son slowly nodded. There were many more stories.

Tom was obviously intelligent, well-educated, and well-traveled, and it took little effort for me to absorb myself in Tom (and vice versa) for several hours. We had shifted from the table and the stylish but uncomfortable ladder-back chairs to the nearby sofa. Without the trace of a seam, the conversation had progressed from past activities to future plans. I told him I was committed to heading up the theater program for Theatre International at Leysin American School in Switzerland that summer. Already I missed him.

Suddenly, magically matching the rest of the evening, as if responding to some cosmic cure, we both stopped regaling each other with the exotic, and I simply gazed into the eyes that seemed to hold so much promise, that seemed to welcome the long-anticipated embrace. The first gentle kiss brought all of the past and future sweeping into the present moment. When I caught my quivering breath, over the throbbing of my heart, I remember thinking, *This can't be happening to me. It is too right, too wonderful.*

There was a short debate – neither of us wanting to separate nor appear too aggressive. Should I stay, or should I go? Early-morning classes beckoned, now only a few hours away. We headed out to the car. By now the streets and highways would be plowed, and I could make it home safely. But fate had other plans. No car. It had been left on the street and consequently towed. So now I had to stay.

And the rest is history.

THE TRICK THAT WOULDN'T LEAVE

by Joseph S. Amster

I'll never forget that first look, hearing an alarm sound inside my head. I remember thinking, *Is this the one I've been looking for?*

Actually, I wish it had been that easy. Our paths had crossed many times that summer. It was only later that we discovered we had been in many of the same places at the same time but were each unaware of the other.

It's as clear to me as the day it happened – "Christopher Street West," the Los Angeles gay pride event, June 1980. After an evening at the festival, I went to a local bathhouse with some friends. The evening had been frustrating; I wasn't connecting with anyone. Then I saw him, leaning against a wall wearing just a towel. Long curly blond hair down to his shoulders, smooth white skin, slim waist and a washboard stomach – my fantasy come to life before my eyes. I tried to make eye contact with him, and I followed him around, but he didn't seem interested, and I was too shy to just go up and talk to him. Eventually I gave up the chase and headed off to the orgy room, consoling myself in the belief that he was just another stuck-up blond.

About a month later I was cruising a park in Laguna Beach, where I met a nice older man who took me back to his house. We had great sex. Although I normally didn't date anyone older than me, we continued to see each other for the rest of that summer. He kept telling me about a friend of his named Vince and all the wild times they had. They used to date but now were just friends.

Vince worked at the bank next to where I worked, so one day I went in to introduce myself. "Oh, you're Charlie's friend," he said. He seemed friendly and cute. He asked me to drop by sometime after work. At the time I didn't realize that he was the guy from the bathhouse.

I was living with my parents that summer, having just come off a disastrous move to Los Angeles. But I had saved enough money and decided to find an apartment in Laguna Beach. While on a break from my job, I ran into a friend who said he could help me find an apartment, but first he had to deliver a message to someone. I tagged along.

We went to an old beach cottage, rang the doorbell, and the door opened. It was Vince. My heart skipped a beat. We immediately recognized each other, and he invited me to come by after work. I took this as a come-on, although he has always said he was just being friendly.

I got off work at 6 and went to his house. I remember feeling a bit disappointed because a parade of his friends kept coming and going through the apartment. I wasn't getting any time alone with him. At least he had a six-month-old fluffy orange kitten named Shibui to play with.

We hadn't kept track of the time, and suddenly, it was 11 p.m. The last of his friends had gone home, and now it was just he and I and the kitty. "Do you want to spend the night?" he asked. I was never one to turn down sex, and it was late and he was blond and thin and cute. How could I say no?

We went into his bedroom and took off our clothes. I had been tricking around a lot that summer and had gotten used to having sex in haste. No emotions – just get in, come, and get out. This was different. It felt very right, like we were made to be together; sensual, slow, gentle lovemaking, where every touch is amplified and felt from the depth of your being. I remember being very turned-on by his body, running my hands over his smooth chest and stomach. It felt natural. We made love for a long time before climaxing and fell asleep in each other's arms. I remember thinking as I drifted off that I had embarked on a new phase of my life.

The next morning he had to get up and go to work but said I could sleep in if I wanted to. He kissed me good-bye and trotted off to work. I stayed for a while, played with Shibui, and finished writing a postcard I had started the day before. I read the card again recently; it says that Vince might be the guy I'd been looking for.

Vince wasn't as quick to agree. He was used to dating a lot of guys, and I became the trick that wouldn't leave. I didn't know any of this at the time and learned later that he was dating five guys when we met.

I had been staying at his place for about three weeks when he told me he had to go to a banking seminar over the weekend. I stayed at my parents' house for a couple of nights – the first time I had been home since Vince and I had met – and went back to his place the following Monday. Vince had brought me flowers, something no one had ever done before. I learned years later that he wasn't at a seminar; he was on a date. He broke it off with the last boyfriend that weekend, and the flowers were to salve his guilt.

Before we settled in for the long haul, there was one more surprise. As I said earlier, I usually dated younger men. I figured from his looks that Vince was at least a couple of years younger than me. He was cashing a check one night, and I glanced down at his driver's license. I was shocked to see that he was older than me. We were born three months apart. So I ended up with an older man after all. I not only gained a lover but a best friend too. We've been together fifteen years now, and I can honestly say that those feelings get stronger as the years go by.

THE CHASE

by J. I. Kessler

I was single again, and two friends wanted me to join them for an evening in gay old Chicago. After several years of a roller-coaster ride that I thought was going to be my happily ever after, I had resolved to remain a bachelor. Although Carlo and Claude were attending school as classmates of my former paramour, they were the only gay men I knew. I had not enjoyed a night out in several years, so their offer was gladly accepted.

Our recipe was simple: Start with an exotic dinner, add a generous portion of dancing, mix flirtatiously with beautiful men, and return home exhausted. I planned on not meeting anyone special since I was uncertain if I would be remaining in the Midwest. My former beau had dragged me across the country and then summarily discarded me, so I didn't intend on settling with anyone in Chicago.

To begin our adventures, we chose a Vietnamese restaurant. Carlo and Claude filled me in on my ex's actions following the end of our relationship. Confirming my suspicions, I learned that he had jumped from our love nest into the arms of an older, wealthier man. Good for him.

We continued on to a dance club in the city's Lakeview neighborhood. Carlo was quickly enamored of the partially clad Adonis who checked our coats; Claude, with everyone else. Having been out of circulation, I felt slightly nervous surveying the terrain. The music and videos were pretty; the men were beautiful. Then I saw him looking at me across the crowded club.

Feeling like the subject of a Rodgers and Hammerstein tune, I pulled Carlo from his vigil of the coat-check god and asked him to confirm that this one was cruising my goods. Carlo verified my guess. My heart skipped a beat. He looked about nineteen, with blond hair and blue-gray eyes. I could not understand why this "kid" was looking at a mature twenty-three-year-old like me. I decided to ignore him and moved elsewhere in the club.

I settled on a stool and engaged myself in a video. Annie Lennox had not finished singing when I felt eyes on me. The kid had followed and was watching me again. He cupped his hand and lit a cigarette like Robert Mitchum in a film noir. Although I'm normally repulsed by smoking, his finesse was intoxicating. I noticed another man looking at the kid, and I felt jealousy flare in my heart. Since I had settled on remaining a bachelor, I moved to a different room.

I leaned against a wall near Claude, who was absorbed in watching dancing bodies. The kid followed me again, and my heart skipped another beat. I whispered to Claude that I was trying an experiment and moved away once more. This time I could not see the kid following me. Feeling foolish, I returned to Claude only to notice through a window that someone who looked like the kid was leaving. I rushed to chase after him, only to find that he had remained by the dance floor. I decided to give up on this cat-and-mouse game, and I positioned myself on the other side of the floor, anticipating his approach. I waited and watched, as did he.

A Madonna tune filled the air. Since dancing to Madonna is an important custom, I swallowed my pride, approached him carefully, introduced myself, and asked him to dance. He consented. We flowed on the floor as song after song swept through the club. After a time, we agreed to stop dancing and talk.

I learned his name was Kert. Originally from downstate, he too had followed a boyfriend to Chicago only to discover that the relationship had soured. He had been out on a blind date but found himself incompatible with his companion. Rather than ruining the remainder of the evening, he had decided to go dancing. He found me attractive, since I appeared Jewish and since I flaunted gay fashion norms by wearing white socks with deck shoes. He also turned out to be just days short of twenty-five. This "kid" was almost two years older than me.

We laughed about my impressions of him and continued to talk about subjects in common: former boyfriends' worthlessness, how we normally avoided bars, interests in musicals, and personal growth. His honesty and intensity were whittling away at my choice to remain single. As we reached an ebb in our conversation, "This Time I Know It's for Real" by Donna Summer blasted over the speakers. We returned to the dance floor, realizing that fate was sending a strong message. Two soul mates were meeting.

The night wore on, and I strategically asked Kert how he intended on returning home. Since I knew public transportation was unreliable at that hour, I offered to drive. He agreed. The comedy of our earlier cat-and-mouse chase was eclipsed by the thirty-minute search for my car on the streets of Lakeview. Claude, Carlo, and I were dizzy from romance, so we could not remember where we had parked.

THE DAY WE MET

My friends recognized the electricity between Kert and me, and when we found the car, they agreed to be dropped off first. The remainder of the night was filled with passion and burgeoning love.

Many years have passed since that night. The dance club is now a leather bar. Claude and Carlo moved on with their lives. I chose not to remain a bachelor but to publicly share my love with Kert with a commitment ceremony twenty months later. We work hard on our relationship and remain deeply dedicated to each other. To this day, however, we still laugh about the circumstances of our meeting.

PEN PALS

by Constantine del Rosario

Montgomery and I will have our six-year anniversary in five months. On that date, as is custom, we will send flowers to our friend Joe, who convinced me to start writing to Montgomery in the first place.

Six years ago Joe and I were both attending the same community college in the San Francisco Bay area. He later transferred to the University of California, Irvine, to finish his degree in dance and, while there, roomed with three other gay men in an on-campus apartment. Joe and I kept in touch by writing, and when he was up north, he'd visit me. Over coffee, he would tell me about his work, school, and one of his roommates, Montgomery, who he thought would be perfect for me. At the time, I had just broken up with a man who lived thirty minutes away from me (what I then considered a long-distance relationship) and told Joe that I had no intention of getting involved with a man who lived seven hundred miles away. "Constantine," Joe replied, "why don't you just write him a letter? What harm could it do?"

As it turned out, I decided to visit my brother in Philadelphia for Thanksgiving that year, and for lack of something to do on the plane, I started writing a letter to Montgomery. In the end it turned out to be a twenty-page travel journal I had to mail in a large manila envelope. I figured the mere sight of a twenty-page letter would be enough to scare him off and that that would be that. Two weeks later an equally long letter arrived from him.

We started writing each other regularly, and since I had decided early on that I was never going to meet this person, I found myself becoming surprisingly candid with him. I started telling him things I would never tell someone I was dating in person. He was also very open with me – and ever so subtly flirtatious, which I found very intriguing and responded to with my own seductive remarks.

I was becoming attracted to a person I had never met. He had no pictures of me, and I had none of him. All Montgomery knew was that I was Asian and of medium build. All I knew was that he was Caucasian, blond, and wore glasses.

After a few months the letters turned into phone calls. First a quick hello to him while talking to Joe, then I was calling Montgomery directly. Now there was a voice – a soft-spoken, polite, and utterly captivating voice – that I wanted to meet.

Joe was having a dance recital of his work performed at the Irvine campus and had invited me to come down. As more of an excuse to meet Montgomery than anything else, I told him I'd love to attend. I was to fly down and stay with the four of them for one week.

Standing, bags in hand, in front of the airport, I waited about ten minutes until I saw Joe's car pull up. I then realized the man sitting next to him in the passenger seat must be the voice on the phone. It was night, and I was barely able to see the face of the man in the gray trench coat as he got out of the car, let me into the backseat, then got back into the passenger seat. Montgomery and I didn't talk much in the car. Mostly, I think, because we were both in a mild state of shock that this moment was actually happening. Joe also has a way of dominating a conversation. Sitting in the backseat listening to Joe talk but paying attention only to the front seat passenger, I noticed his hair wasn't as blond as I thought it would be.

We stopped at a restaurant before going back to the apartment and, for the first time, I was able to see him in full view. He was a bit taller than I thought, about six feet. Though he had a mannish presence, his face was very young-looking. He was, after all, only nineteen, and I was just twenty-three myself. But this face — fair-skinned, smooth, and more attractive than I had imagined — was not exactly the one I had envisioned belonging to the mature and well-spoken man in the letters and on the phone. It was better. Still, over dinner with Joe as chaperon, we still hardly spoke to each other. We would just steal shy glances now and then and agree with whatever Joe was talking about. Had I disappointed him? Why couldn't I make myself talk to him? It was so easy on paper. He even made a special effort to wear his wire-rim glasses that he knew from our correspondence I found irresistible. I couldn't even tell him how cute I thought he looked. I was blowing it.

Back at the apartment, Rito, Joe's roommate, and Dale, Montgomery's roommate, were gone for the evening, and Joe said I could stay in his room or wherever I liked. Joe then quickly went to bed and left Montgomery and me standing alone in the living room. I asked him if I was what he expected.

"Yes," he replied. "Sort of. Maybe a little shorter than I thought."

THE DAY WE MET

The conversation was strained; we were both tired. I said he seemed tense; he said he was a little. I suggested giving him a back rub. At that point we each knew I was trying to seduce him, and he paused for quite some time before saying yes. My two best ways of getting a man are with my cooking and my back rubs.

Once in his room, with the lights low and music in the background, we began to relax. The conversation flowed more easily and the touching seemed to soothe us both. Expectedly, the massaging slowly turned into lovemaking — not the raw animalistic kind but the pure sort that happens only when you're in love. We laughed and talked through the night and reintroduced ourselves to each other now that the initial awkwardness was gone. This was the man I had already fallen in love with before I had ever set eyes on him. With him, I was relaxed. That feeling I had always missed with other men, I found in an upstairs unit of on-campus housing. I was safe.

After about three months of constant letter writing, huge phone bills, and driving back and forth (some trips lasting less than twenty-four hours), we stayed in Southern California for two years, both of us attending UC Irvine. After college, with the cat we adopted along the way, we moved back to the Bay Area, lived in suburbia for a while, then in San Francisco, which is now home.

From that first night together in his apartment, it took me exactly three days to truly fall in love with him. It took Montgomery an additional four days for him to tell me he felt the same way. That seventh day is what we consider our anniversary. That's the day we send flowers to Joe.